D1521258

# The Bomb

# THE BOMB

A Novel

MAKOTO ODA

Translated by D. H. WHITTAKER

Kodansha International
Tokyo and New York

Originally published in Japanese as *HIROSHIMA* by Kodansha Ltd., Tokyo.

Front cover illustration from *Genius loci* by Edgar Ende, copyright © Delfterhof AG, Basel, Switzerland. Reproduced by permission.

Quotations on pp. 36 and 217 are from *Book of the Hopi* by Frank Waters, published by The Viking Press; copyright © 1963 by Frank Waters.

Distributed in the United States by Kodansha International/USA Ltd., 114 Fifth Avenue, New York, New York 10011. Published by Kodansha International Ltd., 17-14 Otowa 1-chome, Bunkyo-ku, Tokyo 112, and Kodansha International/USA.  This is a work of fiction and any resemblance to persons living or dead is purely coincidental. Printed in Japan.

ISBN 4-7700-1481-3 (in Japan)

First edition, 1990

**Library of Congress Cataloging-in-Publication Data**

Oda, Makoto, 1932–
[HIROSHIMA. English]
The bomb / by Makoto Oda; translated by D. H. Whittaker—1st ed.
p. cm.
Translation of: HIROSHIMA.
ISBN 0-87011-981-8 (U.S.)
I. Title.
PL858.D3H5713 1990
895.6'35—dc20

# Foreword

Oda Makoto became well known to the general public in Japan with his 1961 best-seller *Nandemo Mite Yaro (Let's See Everything),* which depicts his experiences as a Fulbright scholar at Harvard University in 1958–1959 and his subsequent world travel. His descriptions of encounters with people of different subcultures and lifestyles while traveling "on the cheap" challenged conventional, often stereotyped, images of foreign countries prevalent in Japan. Oda's insistence on seeing the world through the eyes of the common man and woman has remained a feature of his subsequent work.

In 1964, Oda joined other Japanese writers and scholars in condemning U.S. involvement in Vietnam. He became widely associated with the activities of Beheiren (League of Citizens' Movements for Peace in Vietnam), a loosely organized coalition in which radical groups marched alongside housewives carrying shopping bags. Beheiren held frequent demonstrations and published its own weekly newspaper until it disbanded in 1973.

Since then Oda's activities have spanned a variety of fields, although his anti-war views are still central to his philosophy. He has written numerous novels and social commentaries and contributes regularly to magazines. Translations of his writings have appeared in French, Arabic, Russian, and German, although *The Bomb* is his first full-length work to be published in English. In 1989, Oda was awarded the Lotus Prize of the Africa-Asia Writers' Association, primarily for *The Bomb,* becoming only the third Japanese writer to receive the award.

*The Bomb* was published in Japanese in 1984 under the title *HIROSHIMA*. It is quite different from other accounts of the atomic bombing of that city. The initial setting is a small New Mexican town and the nearby desert of White Sands. This was the testing ground for the atomic bomb, which produced victims at home as well as abroad. A good half of the novel takes place in the United States, incorporating a wide body of material including small-town life, Japanese emigrants and their internment, the legends and world view of the Hopi, and earthquakes. The Japanese setting, too, encompasses the problems of a returnee schoolboy, the plight of Korean forced laborers, the Imperial portrait, the beauty of the Itsukushima Shrine, and of course the devastation wreaked by the Bomb.

Two main themes are discrimination and war, but the relationship is not intended to be causal. The aggressors are at the same time victims however: aggressors to those "below" them and victims of the policies of those "above." It is this ladder of manipulative relationships which Oda attacks in his literary and non-literary activities. His vision of a participatory democracy derives in part from his studies in classical Greek philosophy and literature.

*The Bomb* reflects not only the author's political views but also his personal experiences. He was twelve years old at the time of the air raids over his hometown of Osaka. He also draws upon his observations and experiences during his travels in the U.S. (He recalls, for instance, being mistaken for a Navaho while drinking at a bar near a Hopi reservation.) The richness of these experiences, together with his social concerns and literary skills, warrant this book a wide audience, to which I hope this translation will contribute. I would like to thank in particular the author, Kotoh Koh, Takamatsu Mariko, Mark Williams, Meagan Calogeras of Kodansha International, David

Chesanow, and Jonathan Standing for their help in preparing this English edition. Japanese and Korean names appear with the surnames first, given names last.

D. H. Whittaker
Cambridge, 1990

—το επος—

The whole object of making the weapons is
not to kill people but to find the time for somebody
to find other ways to solve these problems.

Dr. Norris E. Bradbury
Director of Los Alamos Scientific Research Center
1945-1970

# I

The desert was an ideal place for running. Joe frequently ran there, earning himself the nickname "the Runner" from the locals. His work sometimes took him over the road that cut through the desert. He would stop the old Ford truck at the top of the gravel slope that he had decided was the center of the desert, climb out, and take in the faint mauve, snowcapped ranges in the distance. He would relieve himself, change from his thick leather boots into a pair of light canvas shoes, and dart out into the desert.

White Sands, as it was known, was a brown wasteland stretching as far as the eye could see. A few scattered patches of dry grass struggled through the hard, crusty earth. Joe had once brought up a shovel from the ranch to test his strength. He managed to break through the crust, but when he took his hands away the shovel dropped disparagingly to the ground as if to taunt him.

It looked as though some gigantic force had thrown an ocean of rocks over a concrete surface. What strength! And who had scattered those rocks? he wondered. He could feel God when he ran. He sometimes borrowed the Ford to go to church on Sunday morning, inviting cracks about his piety from his boss, Will. He actually went there to meet girls, all decked out in their Sunday best, and arranged dates after the service. After all, you could hardly expect to find God in that poky place, nor in the grating sermon of the asthmatic minister. God was much bigger, like the desert. Not soft like the ruffles of the girls' dresses, but hard like the earth. The Indians living on the edge of the desert probably agreed. For Joe the desert was God.

Last summer he had been caught in a violent thunderstorm, and the desert had offered no refuge. As the rain beating against his cheeks turned to hail, he flung himself facedown on the ground. It may have been the electric atmosphere, but Joe's ears resounded with an uncanny ring. His hair stood on end. This is it, he thought. As he lay in a heap on the ground his left hand began moving of its own accord. It nimbly undid his belt and tossed it away with incredible strength, farther than his right hand could have thrown it. As it landed there was a flash. The lightning hit its target—the eagle buckle he had forgotten was on the belt. When he picked it up the beak of the eagle was dented; the rest of the belt was unscorched.

That was not the only time he had felt God in the desert. Sometimes, when not even a bird could be heard, the parched earth seemed to open its mouth to tell him something. He would stop running and strain his ears to catch the slightest sound, but all around was a heavy silence—the silence of antiquity. A flock of wild geese might fly high overhead and he would watch their wings beating furiously, but not a sound reached him. It was like a silent movie. There they were in the clear sky over the desert, and suddenly they would be gone, as if they had fallen from the sky, exhausted. Even with his twenty-twenty eyesight, Joe couldn't see them. Yes, the desert did seem too vast to fly over.

At such times, something more striking than the thunderstorm told him that the desert was God. Something indescribably vast, like the whole desert itself, would press into him, cutting his breath. If he had succumbed and fallen then, he might indeed have seen God. Instead he would start running, bounding over the concrete surface. His body would become strangely light, as if bounced about like a hurled rock. Who did scatter those rocks?

Joe worked hard, too, as a ranch hand. He may not have been as skilled as Will, but he could manage the horses pretty well. He did well at the rodeos, surprising some of the veterans with his crazy feats. But his real steed on the ranch was the Ford truck, more than fifteen years old now and showing signs of wear. If it didn't start it just needed a thump on the dashboard: "You heap of junk, do as you're told or I'll sell you," he would snarl, and off it went. It was still a solid machine—able to handle the ranch and send stones flying in the desert. Joe felt as if it were a part of himself. "You should see your face," Will bantered once when he watched Joe driving over the desert. It was the same face Joe had when he was running—crying and laughing at the same time. He took a mirror with him the next time. Will was right.

There were always a few bullets rolling around under the driver's seat, and a shotgun hung on a frame beside the steering wheel. There were no police around. They had to look after themselves. Will had a special police license that meant he could arrest thieves he found on his ranch. He could also shoot if he had to.

After two years of living together, Joe knew Will was pretty good-natured, but that he could be implacable when he had to be. He didn't like mistakes at work, and although it didn't happen so much now, when Joe had first started working there, Will often came down hard on him. But soon he would silently be offering Joe a cigarette. Will was just into his sixties, stout and broad- shouldered, with few signs of deterioration. He had no wife or children, or none at the ranch at least.

"They say you've got three kids," Joe probed once. He had heard a rumor at the Golden Eagle. Above the entrance of the local bar was a carving of an eagle, its wings raised, from which the bar took its name. Will glowered back and snapped, "Mind your own business."

His name was William MacDowell, a common enough name, but his body and face were impressively large. It was silver now, but the golden hair that had covered his body was definitely from his Scandinavian mother's side. His father's side was Scottish. His deep-set eyes were a penetrating blue, the color of the Scandinavian fiords. His forefathers must have stared at them for years, Joe thought when he saw some photos in Will's National Geographic. When he said so, Will just snorted. He didn't say, "Mind your own business."

Joe had been living at Will's ranch, thirty minutes from town, for two years, since he was seventeen years old. Those two years were like ten years to an older man. He had already become a competent ranch hand. He strode around in his simple but tough handmade boots, shoulders slightly stooped, ready for anything. He could subdue a rampaging horse in seconds. That's how Will worked too. Joe had just picked up everything from him. When they walked together they looked like father and son. Perhaps Will thought so as well. He started calling Joe "son"—when he was in a good mood, of course.

Like the ranchers in the Westerns, he didn't talk much. Kind underneath but hard with his workers. No one had ever stayed more than three months before Joe came. Al, the gas station owner, had told Joe about the job. Al was a local but had worked his way from New York to San Francisco. Larry, the owner of the Golden Eagle, called him a drifter. Joe came from about a hundred miles away, over the state border. By chance he stopped for gasoline one day and, while Al was cleaning the window, asked half-jokingly if he knew of any jobs going. "Yeah, I reckon I do . . ." Al grinned. After they became friends he told Joe the rest of the sentence: ". . . but I wonder for how long."

Both of Joe's parents were dead. He had left home to find work and a place to live because he felt he was becoming a burden on his brother's family. "You sure picked a place, didn't you. " Al shook his head. "I didn't think you'd last three days." Two or three times, after a quarrel, he had thought about leaving. But he knew deep down he was in the wrong. Will only bawled at him when he was doing a bad job. If he was trying and bungled, Will just gave him a look but didn't say anything. Whatever else you could say about Will, he was a great rancher. Joe knew that after two days working with him. I'll watch him and I'll learn everything he can teach me, he thought. I'll become a man by learning from a man. Men can be stubborn, so I've got to be too. When Will called him "son", Joe never called him "Dad." He was Will or, when he was being pigheaded, Mr. MacDowell.

It was quite a small ranch—about sixty head of cattle, ten horses, twenty sheep, and a hundred acres of watermelons. Two men could usually do the work, except at harvest time, when they took on some Indians from the reservation or Mexicans from over the border.

The problem with the Indians was that they liked their drink. They would get drunk and start pulling knives and the like. The Mexicans were much quieter, but maybe they just kept everything bottled up inside, because they could really explode. One started brandishing a jackknife at Will once. Sometimes the immigration people came round and took some of them away. "Turn a few over to the immigration people and you won't have that kind of trouble," Larry was always saying, but Will never would.

The Mexicans didn't even seem to mind when they were taken away. "We'll be back," they said, and next season there they were, back at the ranch again. The ones who could speak

English had a Southern drawl, but others never bothered to learn any English, no matter how many times they came. They just shrugged their shoulders and grinned.

Will and Joe did most of the work, and that was what tied them together. They got up at five in the morning and worked hard until long after the sun had gone down over the distant ranges. Most of the day they worked in silence, taking care of the cows, chasing lazy Indians and Mexicans back to work in the fields, making their meals, settling disputes—there was plenty of work to do. If the truck broke down they couldn't call a mechanic to come; they had to fix it themselves. Will was an expert repairman. Once Joe had had a careless accident with the Ford. Will spent five hours fiddling with it and got it going again.

"Incredible. You should open a garage." Joe anticipated the feigned punch and stepped back.

"You'd make a pretty good boxer yourself."

Will once caught Joe masturbating. The desert did that to him. The first time was after he met an Indian girl out there. She must have been about thirteen or fourteen, but she had hair like you see in the Westerns, hanging down around both sides of her face. The setting sun made it shine a lustrous black. Perhaps the passing shower had made it wet, or perhaps it naturally shone like that. She wasn't wearing Indian clothes, just a coarse dress with long woollen socks and handmade moccasins. Her father or brother had probably stayed up one night making them for her.

"Hi!" He waved cheerfully, but was greeted with a hostile stare. Her expression was hard, her body poised, on the alert. It was slender, like a sharp knife. If he showed any sign of attack it would stab at him desperately. No doubt she sensed his seething desire. Her mother had probably told her that white men attack Indian girls. There were some children in the Indian village with different faces, the result of assaults by white men like him.

His desire became a big, hard lump inside his body, thrusting its way up. He wasn't thinking of using her body to release his lust, as she no doubt thought. Nor was it as it had been with the white girls he had known—a little talk, alcohol, dancing, then naked on a motel bed. He just wanted to lie with her on the pebble-strewn desert, roll about like frisky dogs copulating, and come together naturally. He wanted to embrace and feel their bodies unite. Sex was not the right word for it. He wanted something more natural, a union which was beyond words.

He watched her as she slowly walked away, her shiny black hair swaying from side to side. She walked with a slight limp, and even that excited him in a peculiar way. Dusk was drawing near, but there was still some strength in the evening sun. He stood there consoling himself and at his climax glanced up to see the girl's tiny figure disappearing and the rocks shining a brilliant red. That wasn't when Will saw him. He sometimes returned to the same place. At first the image of the girl came to him, but now he just consoled himself. It had become the natural thing to do in the desert. Then one time he looked up and saw Will standing there.

"Son," he said, as usual, but his tone of voice was different. "The Japs have attacked Pearl Harbor. . . ." He looked troubled and carried on, almost to himself. "Pearl Harbor—that's the naval base in Hawaii. West of Honolulu—"

"You came all the way out here to tell me that?" Joe could sense there was something else.

"No, not only that," he mumbled. "Ken came around." That was not good news. No, it might actually be good news for Will right now. Deep down he had been both resisting and waiting for it at the same time. Joe could see the uncertainty around his sunken eyes.

Ken—Kenneth E. Rose—was the biggest rancher in those parts, and one of the biggest entrepreneurs. He was a real businessman, with a loud voice and a booming laugh. He was expanding his business and everyone knew he wanted Will's ranch. It was a fact that things had not been going well at the ranch for the past year or two. The age of the small farmer was giving way to mass production, and there was no turning back the clock. More important, Will was getting on, his asthma was getting worse, and he had begun to believe in the signs of the times. "When a man feels it's the end, it is the end," Joe remembered him muttering when he first went to work at the ranch. There was more resignation in his voice when he said that now.

In the last few months, especially, he had aged. This could be his chance to retire somewhere down around Florida, where the climate was good. The more active someone is, the more he wants to throw it all in when he becomes tired. Joe was active himself, so he could understand Will's wavering.

Sometimes he tried to imagine Will in retirement. A little bit of carpentry, some gardening, perhaps. Always a hard worker and very particular, Will would take even such pastimes seriously. Instead of a big tractor, he would tend the grass with a small mower. If the mood took him, he might make a table or some cupboards, or take a shotgun out for pheasants the way he sometimes did at the ranch. And then, he would put on his glasses to read *National Geographic* and fall asleep within five minutes, fifty years of work-weariness heeded at last. *National Geographic* was a good sleeping pill, even now. For some reason, if you go to any rancher's house, you'll find some copies in the magazine rack in the living room. No one seems to read them very much. Perhaps they think they'll read them when they retire — take them to Florida and read them beside the warm sea.

Joe was determined not to let that happen to him, but sometimes he could see himself in the figure of Will asleep with reading glasses on and the magazine spread across his lap. Before that, though, he would find himself a woman, get married, and make a home. They'd have children, of course, and the children would grow up. When they got to be as old as he was now, well, he would think about what to do then. Retirement would come after all that. The future lay in front of him, wide open like the desert.

"So, did you decide to sell?" Joe got straight to the point. Like Will, he didn't like beating around the bush. He didn't like putting on airs either. It sometimes got him into trouble, but a person's character can't change easily. There was nothing wrong with calling a spade a spade.

"Yes, I decided to sell." Will put his corncob pipe in his mouth and changed his tone. "He said he would keep you on. He wants you because you know what's going on."

"I don't feel like staying," Joe shot back. "I wouldn't get along with him." Ken wasn't all that bad, and Joe didn't object too strongly to his acquisitive ways. As a businessman, he was reasonably generous. Joe simply didn't like the man and the feeling was probably mutual.

They had tangled in the bar once. Both had been drinking, and Ken insinuated that Joe's hair was black because he had Indian blood in him and that because Indians were related to Asians, maybe Joe was related to those buck-toothed, squint-eyed, yellow-faced Japs. Joe was slim but tall, with plenty of muscle on him. Potbellied, middle-aged Ken would be no match for him. But Ken had influence in the town. If Joe stirred up trouble, Ken might laugh it off, but his friends wouldn't. Leaning on Joe, Ken knew that. The gauntlet had been thrown. Joe braced himself, but at that moment, as if by divine intervention, the heavy wooden door opened and Will appeared. "Son, you look happy tonight. Have you found a nice blonde or something?" he teased Joe and waltzed up between them. "How about you?" he said turning to Ken.

"I don't wanna work for Ken," Joe repeated as they stood in the middle of the desert. Will nodded.

"Where will you go—your brother's place? Knowing you, I guess you won't want to go back there."

"Damned right. I think I'll go west."

"Why west?"

"I just feel like there's something there."

"If you go too far . . ." Will said mischievously. "Don't go as far as Jap country."

"Maybe I will. I suppose healthy people like me will get called up anyway."

"I hate to say it, son, but I think you're right" Will nodded. He didn't say anything patriotic about going to kill the Japs to protect freedom. If he had been Ken, who had his eye on a public office, he might have, but Will was a man of few words, and couldn't pretend even if he had wanted to. "Ken was asking"—again he spoke haltingly —"why that youngster at my place—that's you—is always running around out here. There's an Indian living out there who ran in an Olympic marathon. Maybe you've got the same idea, but there's a war on. 'This is no time for Olympics.' That's what he said. But it made me think. Why are you doing all this marathon training?"

"I'm not training for any marathon." Joe turned the other way and stared across the desert. "I'm just running. Like the coyotes." Once, in fact, a coyote had raced past him while he was running. It didn't look like anything was chasing it, or it chasing anything. It was just running, as if from this world into the next. Its beautiful fur caught the evening rays, and it flew past like a silver streak.

"Son, if you get into the war, you make sure you come back. Countries will be there whether you're alive or dead. And you live whether there are countries or not. So you've got to stay alive whatever happens. A friend told me that once." Will had been in the last war, but he never talked about it. Someone said that he was one of only five in his unit who came back. "What do you think?"

"Yeah." Joe turned away again. "I'll come back."

"Good."

"Your friend, the one who wanted to stay alive, what happened to him?"

"He was killed. Had his head shot off."

"Let's get going," Joe ventured, after a moment's awkward silence. As they started to walk back, Joe suddenly stopped in his tracks. He thought he saw another coyote racing across the desert— toward the next world. The silver glint lingered in his eyes.

Joe didn't know it, but he had a secret admirer. Her name was Peggy. She had only just entered fourth grade, but she was a precocious girl and already considered herself a young lady. In her dreams she and Joe were the same age. Sometimes she was a little older. At night their secret love story unfolded above her pillow, but it usually didn't last very long. The dream ended happily with their marriage in the local church, and she would slip into a peaceful slumber, not to awake until the next morning.

She had first met Joe at church one Sunday. A tall, slim young man had sat down next to her. He was with Will, and since Will and her father, Elzie, knew each other, they were introduced. Trying to be ladylike (she must have seen this in the movies— the local women were not so pretentious), she held out her hand. She was delighted when instead of laughing at her Joe bent down and lightly kissed it. She could still feel his lips tickling the back of her hand.

Every Sunday since then they met at church. She didn't hold out her hand, so he didn't bend down to kiss it, but he would give her a wink of acknowledgment and sometimes venture something like "How are you today, my pious young lady." She never missed church and always tried to think about God. She was relieved whenever she saw Joe at church. Anyone she liked should of course be a believer. God forbid that he become like Al at the gas station. "He's never set foot inside a church. He's an atheist, a red," her father always said. She knew Al was a friend of Joe's; in a town of fifteen hundred people, everyone knew everything about everyone.

Peggy had also heard that Joe went running in the desert beyond the hills west of town. In fact, Will had introduced him as "the famous Runner." She decided he must be training for the Olympics like Chuck. Chuck was an Indian, the hero of his tribe. He had run in the Olympic marathon, winning a bronze medal the second time. That was thirty years ago, when Chuck was famous even in the white man's world. About the only other person from the town who had been to Europe, in addition to Chuck and Will, was Mr. Griggs, the owner of the drugstore. He had been to France in the last war, where a mine blew his right leg off below the knee. No wonder he was the grumpiest man in town.

But Chuck had been there twice, and not for sightseeing or for war. Both times he went as a representative of the U.S.A.

He came back with a bronze for the honor of his country. Some of the old- timers could recall the hordes of reporters coming down from New York and Washington to the reservation, and even to the town, for their stories. Chuck had first come there when he was young to find work. His boss, who had done track and field at high school, got him started. At least that's what his boss told the reporters, but it was all a long time ago. Chuck moved from the reservation with some kin several years ago and they built some shacks on the edge of the desert, close to Will's ranch. On occasion he would come into town, tottering down the main street, past the bank, Mr. Griggs' drugstore, the small supermarket, and Larry's Golden Eagle. Now he looked like one of the old Indians who did seasonal work or odd jobs to fill his belly. Not a vestige of the old "hero" remained.

Peggy had heard about Chuck from Laura, who had come from one of the shacks to be a live-in housemaid in Peggy's home. About three years older than Peggy, she had long, shiny black hair that bounced as she walked. She had a slight congenital limp, worked hard, and said little, but Peggy felt she was always on her guard. She was tall and thin, like Peggy. "When you two stand together you look like two sticks," Peggy's father teased her. It wasn't being called a stick that she objected to, but being put in the same category as an Indian.

"That's Chuck," Laura declared proudly, pointing him out in the street. All Peggy could see was an old man in a dirty sweater, limping along like a convalescent, like Laura. He had a big frame but only the frame was left, a skeleton of a big man. "He's our hero." She launched into his history, almost oblivious of Peggy. Peggy was taken aback, not at the story itself but at the way Laura was talking so fast, so eloquently, as if she were possessed by the hero's spirit. And stories about Olympic bronze medals in far-off Europe were just too removed from the life of their little town to mean anything to her.

"I don't believe it," she said. That hobbling old man couldn't possibly have been a marathon runner.

"But it's true," Laura insisted, looking sadly at Peggy.

Naturally associating Joe with running, Peggy mentioned his name. A sweetheart's name is something you want to keep locked up inside you, but at the same time you need to share your secret. "He's also 'the Runner,'" she said as nonchalantly as she could. She felt a weight lifted off her mind, and felt herself going red. Laura hadn't known Joe was the Runner, but she knew he lived on a ranch near their settlement, and that he sometimes ran on the desert. She mentioned meeting him there once. "He must have looked great," Peggy sighed. She hadn't seen him running yet, but she knew he had to look good.

Laura laughed evasively and continued her story. The land around the reservation was deeply furrowed, the plains suddenly giving way to deep-cut gorges and soaring rocky mountains. Chuck lived on top of one, high up, like a citadel. From the time he could walk, Chuck had run up and down the mountains. He hadn't learned to run after he came into town to work, Laura said, staring at Peggy. He was already running, in wind, rain, snow, in hail as big as a dog's head; he always ran. Sometimes he ran on the desert, too, but he didn't go there in a truck. He ran there and he ran back as part of his training.

"Yes, but he's not like that now, is he?" Peggy said, cutting Laura's eulogy short. "First of all, he's almost a cripple." Her caustic remark had a double edge, aimed at Laura, too, who had dared to make fun of Joe. Joe was young and strong, not a cripple, and he ran on the desert almost every day.

Laura was hurt but she would not let it show. A sparkle returned to her eyes as she went on to talk about her brother Ron. Ron was two years younger than Peggy and an amazingly fast runner. The tribe expected him to follow in Chuck's footsteps. When their family recently went back to the reservation for a festival, the top runners had raced from the desert to the altar on top of the rocky mountain. Ron turned in a good performance, and when they got back home and told everyone of Ron's exploits, even Chuck squinted and laughed: "Ron, you are sure to get a gold medal in the Olympics." He pulled him over and rubbed his cheeks. From then on, Ron went running every day, come what may. He even ran into town sometimes, which was hard for Peggy to believe, since he was so small. She had seen him once when he came to visit his sister. The two legs sticking out of his grubby cutoff shorts looked anything but sturdy. She's lying, thought Peggy, and she felt somehow relieved.

"Indians are liars," Peggy's mother always said, and Laura had just confirmed it. Her mother also said that you never knew what "those people" were thinking. "Those people" included Indians, Negroes, Chinese, and especially Japs. Peggy's parents were locals, but they had lived for a long time in southern California. An eye accident had forced Elzie to give up his job as a factory inspector, and they came back a year ago so that he could make a new start as an insurance agent. They weren't outsiders, but Larry managed to annoy him by saying that no one would care if California sank into the Pacific in an earthquake. Their small town in California had been a Jap town. In the streets, shops, kindergartens, schools, the Japs were everywhere. It had seemed as if whites, like Peggy's family, were a minority.

When the talk got on to the subject of Japs, Elzie pointed out that Alaska was once joined to Siberia, and thus Japs and Indians were related. Peggy couldn't really take that in either. She knew where Alaska was but had never heard of Siberia. And the Japs in her Californian town were small and stooped, not like the towering figures that strode around the desert with feather headdresses. (She had never actually seen any Indians like that— the Indians you saw in town were a pretty motley lot). Take their old neighbor Mr. Nakata, for example, who ran a small drugstore. When she went there to buy candy he would smile at her, displaying his mouth full of crooked teeth, and when she left he would almost fall over bowing.

The Nakatas and her family were not close, but they were neighbors and maintained neighborly relations. It wasn't fair for her mother to decide from their few encounters that Japs were liars, but it was certainly true that you couldn't tell what Mr. Nakata was thinking. Was it because neither he nor Mrs. Nakata—Kunie is what he called her—could speak much English? Or because they were naturally quiet? Or maybe because they were always grinning when she met them? What absolved them was the youngest of their three sons. He was two years younger than Peggy, about the same age as Laura's brother Ron. He was bright and sharp, like any American boy, and always gave straight answers. He seemed to make a good impression on everyone. Peggy's mother remembered him long after she forgot about Mr. and Mrs. Nakata and the other two boys. Even her father, who rarely had any interest in his neighbors, remembered him. When she mentioned Tommy he nodded approvingly. "Ah, him, the Jap boy."

"He's gone back to Japan," he recalled one day.

"Why?" Peggy asked. Her father seemed surprised by the question.

"Why? He's a Jap, isn't he? It's natural for Japs to go back to their own country."

"Has Mr. Nakata gone too?"

"No, only Tommy. He always talked about wanting to send his son to school in Japan." Peggy didn't bother to ask why again.

"Where did he go? To Tokyo?" It was the only city in Japan she knew.

"I forget what he called it. It started with an *H*. Most Japs in America come from there."

"So Tommy went back there," Peggy said thoughtfully.

"That's right. Now let's go on inside." Father and daughter had been talking outside in the sun-dappled empty plot of land next to their house. The war between Japan and America had already started, but the topic had not entered their conversation. Like the Olympics in Europe, war was something too remote from life in their town. Peggy tried to imagine Tommy in his town in Japan going to school, but all she could conjure up was a blank, white picture.

When Will and Joe arrived at Ken's place in their old Ford truck, Ken was up on the roof, shoveling snow. He was never happy unless he was doing something. With him were two workers, one a middle-aged white man, the other a Mexican. Joe parked the truck by the garage, and as they walked over, Ken raised his shovel in greeting. The snow was dazzling in the morning sun, and the red roof emerging from under its white cover provided a striking contrast. Before Will could wave back, Joe called out, "It's the Japs. We've come to take over your house."

"Never seen a white Jap before." Ken came down to lead them inside, but Joe hesitated.

"This white Jap'll stay out here and shovel snow so you don't end up with a bomb on you." Joe snatched the shovel from Ken and shinned nimbly up the ladder.

Ken looked after him in bemusement and then turned to Will. "Come in," he said, and led him to the porch facing an enormous courtyard pool. There was no water in it, since it was winter, but in summer Ken and his two children used it almost every day.

"Thanks," Will said, following him in. He appreciated Joe's consideration. He was going to sign the contract of sale. Somewhere inside he felt it was a document of surrender, and no doubt so did Joe. His defiant attitude had made it clear that he didn't want to watch. He had a rough edge but essentially a good heart, Will thought, especially since talk had begun about selling the ranch. Joe didn't approve of the sale, and no matter what terms Ken offered, he wasn't going to stay on. Like Will, once he decided something, he wasn't likely to change his mind. Joe didn't try to dissuade Will, and Will could sympathize with Joe. "This is your ranch. When it's Ken's, it'll be no place for me to work." Will remembered those words.

There was no ceremony in the signing of the contract between the two ranchers. It was done by the blazing fire in the living room, and Will actually felt a sense of relief when it was over. Ken's wife, a plump, middle-aged woman with red hair, brought in some tea. Looking at her, Will felt his emotions stir. His wife had also had red hair. But that was a long time ago. He watched calmly as she poured the steaming tea from a white china teapot and placed a cup before him. The three of them talked for a while, then she excused herself and left, leaving the spacious room to the two of them. Ken talked non-stop about the stock sale the following Saturday, and Will realized he had missed his chance to leave when Ken's wife went out. But he also felt that if he had left at that moment, he would be placing the ranch in Ken's hands. The date for the transfer of title was set for next May, still five months away, and until then he would receive installments from Ken, get his debts paid off, and plan his future.

"It wouldn't be right to chase you out now, would it?" Ken said benevolently, but it wouldn't have done him any good to get the ranch in winter anyway. It would be cheaper and easier to let Will and Joe take care of it than having to employ a caretaker.

"I reckon I should go when the weather starts getting better," Will replied, nodding.

They could hear Joe chatting with the white man and the Mexican outside on the roof. Sunlight streamed through the porch window, adding to the warmth of the fire crackling behind them. They took off their sweaters as they continued their talk. The stock sale next Saturday was the biggest in the area for horses. Ken proudly handed Will a leaflet from his desk, as if he were the sponsor of the event.

"But I guess you're not interested. . . . You're retiring to Florida."

Will nodded. He wasn't interested. He felt at that moment that their positions had been reversed, for his nod was one of accomplishment. Joe's voice drifted in again, something about a rattlesnake he'd seen while running on the desert. It had tried to get him, a big one about six feet long.

"That's good thing," the Mexican said in broken English.

"You reckon? I thought it was pretty bad news," Joe laughed. "What's good for a Mexican is not good for an American. Rattlesnakes don't understand English."

"That joker don't understand Spanish either."

"That joker, that's a good one," the white man laughed. "Was it male or female?"

"It was coming after me, so it must have been female—a beauty at that."

"He . . ." Ken stopped and listened to the conversation on the roof. "He doesn't want to work for me?"

"Whether he wants to or not, he's going to be called up soon. If someone as fit as him doesn't get called up, there must be something wrong."

"He's still running?" Ken asked, with a hint of derision in his voice. "Trying to get to the Olympics. . . . It's wartime now. Those damned Japs came and started it. . . ." The conversation switched to the talk of the town, about how dastardly the Japs were for springing a surprise attack on Pearl Harbor. Will thought so, too, and their conversation livened up. It was as if they agreed about something for the first time in their lives. "We've got to have it out with those bastards."

Will nodded. "If I were a bit younger, I'd sign up myself."

"I wonder if it'll be over quickly."

"I've a feeling it will be. Then . . ." Will motioned to the roof.

"Then he'll start running again," Ken chuckled. "When I was a kid one of my classmates was always running. He was skinny, with long legs, but he was fast. That was when I was at boarding school." Ken had been to an agricultural school in a small town in the north of the state. Will knew about the town because one of his workers had come from there, a Hispanic with jet-black hair. "What have you got up there?" he had asked him once. "Mountains and valleys" was the reply.

"And what happened to him? Did he get to the Olympics?"

Ken shook his head. "He became a policeman. I guess his long legs were good for catching thieves." It was a poor joke, maybe even a lie, and Will didn't attempt to suppress a yawn.

"He couldn't have been something more original— a senator or something?"

"One of my classmates became a professor. I can't remember, but he was teaching at a university."

"What kind of professor?"

"Physics maybe. Well, whatever, beyond the understanding of the likes of us. Anyway, he became famous. He was a Jew."

"All scholars are Jews," said Will. Those words seemed to fan Ken's dislike of Jews, for he let out a tirade of invective. The worst people in the world were the Japs, followed by the Jews. Both were sneaky, and both thought only of themselves. Hitler threw the Jews out to make them come and ruin this country. While Ken was rattling on, the phone rang in the corner of the room. He looked at it as if he were making up his mind about something, then slowly got up to take it.

"It's for Joe, from your place. You can take it if you like." Ken held out the receiver. It was from the Mexican they had taken on to help rebuild the barn. His English was even worse than that of the Mexican on the roof.

"He army."

"He—who's he?" It only took Will an instant to realize that the Mexican meant Joe.

Joe's draft notice had come.

"He's joining army." Will's English was strange now. Ken was startled, but only for a moment. "That's good. He can go in our place and kill the Japs," he said cheerfully.

On New Year's Day before sunup, Ron Muchuck ran from his house over the slopes toward the immense sandstone landmark where his uncle, Chuck Paweki, was waiting. His breath was white in the fresh air. Chuck had come in his battered car. The landmark looked like a giant with a big head, poised to move at any time. It was about twice as high as Chuck and four times the width of a fat man. There were other lumps of sandstone dotting the desert, but this one was much bigger. When Ron suggested meeting there, Chuck had nodded and said, "I used to go running around that rock."

Ron could see the rock from a distance, and as he ran it seemed to move, like a white giant staggering around in the gloom. The dark figure standing beside it, with arms folded, seemed to be swaying too.

"Chuck," Ron called, addressing his uncle as a friend. He called twice, and finally, as if roused from sleep, Chuck turned to look at him. He was standing sideways to the wind.

"Happy New Year." Ron tried to sound like an adult.

"Happy New Year," Chuck replied solemnly. "You did well to get up so early. Did you get up by yourself?"

"Of course," Ron replied proudly. "Mom and Dad are still sleeping. And Laura too."

"They're all sleepyheads." Chuck's expression warmed, his smile fanning out into countless wrinkles that still managed to exude a childlike innocence. "It looks like it's going to be okay this year." He looked up at the sky over the desert, still pale but cloudless.

They had gone out onto the desert at dawn last New Year, too, although they had met in a different place then. A heavy cloud cover had hidden the sunrise. They waited for it to break but it got thicker and then started to rain. "We wait until next year," Chuck said emphatically. "We must come here again then, Ron."

He was going to explain to Ron about the Creation and the legends handed down in his tribe. "You're growing up; it's time you know them. You will be carrying the honor of our tribe," he said proudly after Ron had just returned from the race held at the reservation. One day he, too, would run in the Olympics. Two months later, when the first rays peeped over the desert on New Year's Day, would be the best time to tell him, if it was clear weather, Chuck had thought then.

If the first rays of sun could not be seen over the desert horizon, he would not tell the story. The sun was their father, and the story of the Creation should be told under his light. The sun was their father and the earth was the mother, the earth and the corn that came from it—he often used the two synonymously. Ron knew that much already.

This year the sun was certain to appear. The desert was still veiled in darkness, but the signs of dawn were already in the sky.

"In the beginning was Taiowa. There was nothing else and no one else." Chuck began to speak slowly, his arms still folded, eyes looking intently far out into the desert as if he were observing a distant moving object. "There was no earth, no sea, no mountains, no rivers." He paused and, after a moment, continued.

"Just a void. A boundless and formless void. The maker of the void was the Creator, Taiowa. Then he made Sótuknang. He said to Sótuknang: 'I made you. I made you to carry out my plans. I am your uncle.' " Chuck paused to look at Ron. His face seemed to Ron to be that of Taiowa himself, larger than normal and very noble. He continued: " 'Nephew,' said Taiowa, 'Go and make a world out of this void with a form and a center.'

"And Sótuknang made a world with a form and center, according to Taiowa's instructions. When he had finished he turned to Taiowa and asked, 'Is this good?'

"'It is good,' Taiowa said, praising his nephew. 'Now I want you to go again and make water.'

"So Sótuknang made water, and poured it over the face of the world until it was half solid and half water. Then the nephew said to his uncle, 'I want you to go and check with your own eyes what I have done.' 'It is very good, but there is more work to do,' Taiowa said. 'What is that?' the nephew asked. 'Make air, and fill the world with it.'

"And so the world was filled with air and at the same time the wind began to move slowly. Taiowa was happy. 'You have done very well. But your work is not finished yet. Now you must make life. Life and movement.'

"So Sótuknang went to the First World. It was called the First World because Sótuknang was later to destroy it and create the Second World, the Third World, and the Fourth World. The present world, the one in which you and I are living, is the Fourth World.

"In the First World Sótuknang made the Spider Woman. When the Spider Woman was born she asked Sótuknang, 'Why did you create me?' Sótuknang answered, 'Look around you. This is the world we have made. There is shape and substance. There is direction. There is time; a beginning and an end. The world is not formless, but there is no life yet. There is still no movement, no joy. There is no sound of joy. What is life without movement and sound?'

"Following his instructions, the Spider Woman took some clods of earth and mixed them with her saliva. She made two beings and covered their heads with a white substance. This was the substance of creative wisdom. The Spider Woman sang the Song of Creation, and took away the covering to reveal a pair of twins. 'Why did you create us? Why are we here?' they asked. She spoke to the twin on the right: 'You, Pöqánghoya, go around the world and make it fit for living things. That is why you are here.' To the twin on the left, she said, 'You, Palöngawhoya, go around the world and create sound. You shall be called Echo. All sounds will echo the Creator.'

"Pöqánghoya traveled around the world, making the high places into solid mountains. The low places he made firm but pliable enough so that those placed there would be able to use her and call her their mother.

"Palöngawhoya traveled around the world making sound. He made all vibrating things resonate along the world's axis, from pole to pole, so the world became an instrument of sound. All messages were conveyed by sound, and sound existed for the praise of Taiowa, the Creator. 'This is your voice,' Sótuknang said to Taiowa. 'It is very good,' Taiowa replied.

"When the work was finished, Pöqánghoya was sent to the north pole, and Palöngawhoya to the south pole, in order to maintain the rotation of the world. Pöqánghoya was given the power to keep the earth firm. Palöngawhoya was given the power to maintain the quiet movement of the wind, give sound to the earth, and make the ground tremble.

"The Spider Woman then made trees, bushes, and flowering plants, covering the earth with them, giving them all life and a name. She then made birds and animals, fashioning their shapes from the soil. She covered their heads with the white substance and sang the Song of Creation. She placed some of the birds and animals to her right and some to her left, some in front and some behind, and directed them to spread out all over the earth.

"With land, plants, birds, and animals, the world was beautifully radiant. Sótuknang said to Taiowa, 'Behold the world we have made.' 'It is very good,' replied Taiowa. 'It is now time to complete the plan: to make human life.' "

The desert had gradually been getting lighter. The dark, expressionless expanse of land rolled into relief, and hues of colors and melodies of birds now filled the void.

"It is almost morning." Chuck suddenly stopped and looked around, adding emphasis to his words. Ron looked around too. He saw two or three strangely shaped sandstone blocks, a little smaller than the one next to them, one of which looked just like a coyote running.

Chuck fixed his gaze on the northern sky. Ron was not sure why, since the sun would rise from the east, but he did the same. All that could be seen above the desert was the cold, clear sky. After standing motionless for a while, Chuck turned to Ron again.

"So the Spider Woman finally made man. She took some earth, this time of four colors—yellow, red, white, and black. She mixed the clumps with her saliva, molded them, and gave to them the white cap of creative wisdom. Then she sang the Song of Creation. She removed the covering to reveal four men, exactly like Sótuknang, each with a different color of skin. Then she made four women modeled on herself. Again the color of their skins was different."

Chuck kept his eyes on the northern sky and began to chant in a low voice:

*The dark purple light rises in the north,*
*A yellow light rises in the east.*
*Then we of the flowers of the earth come forth*
*To receive a long life of joy.*

He stopped. "Look!" Instinctively, Ron looked at the northern sky. It was a faint, dark purple, just as Chuck had sung. "It is now *qöyangnuptu.*" Ron nodded. They were in the first stage of *qöyangnuptu*, which would be followed by *síkangnuqa* and *tálawva*, the three stages in man's birth. "The men and women the Spider Woman had made started moving, but their foreheads were wet and there was a soft spot on their heads."

"The soft part is called *kópavi,*" Ron declared, showing the spot. This was the gateway from the inside of man directly to the Creator. When man was born, Taiowa breathed in the breath of life through his *kópavi.*

"Now it is *síkangnuqa.*" As Chuck spoke, yellow beams tinged with red lit up the eastern sky. "It was during *síkangnuqa* that Taiowa breathed the breath of life into the four men and four women that the Spider Woman had made." Chuck's voice was getting hoarse. "And during *síkangnuqa,* Taiowa breathes the breath of life into every child that is born. That's how you were born, too, Ron"

"And you, too, uncle." Ron felt a strong, vital energy welling up inside him.

"Look!" Chuck said again.

The red tinge had gradually intensified. Suddenly a bright flash of light shot over the desert into their eyes. "Sunrise! *Tálawva!*" they shouted together.

"*Tálawva* is the red light of the third stage," Chuck added, after a momentary pause. All around them the birds, which had been quiet, suddenly flew up into the air in a chorus of sound and movement.

As the red shape on the horizon grew larger and more dazzling, Ron felt a current of warm air envelop him as if someone had just lit a fire. Chuck turned to the rays coming from the horizon as if to dry his forehead, wet from dew, and continued telling Ron about the four men and four women, yellow, red, white, and black, that the Spider Woman had made. "Their foreheads gradually dried, and the soft part, *kópavi,* began to harden.

"The open gateway that connected them with Taiowa, the *kópavi,* was closed. The same thing happened when I was born, when you were born, and when anyone is born. With each breath the gateway rises and falls, sending signals to Taiowa. When we die the gateway opens and connects us with Taiowa again.

"Behold, Taiowa!" As the sun rose above the horizon

Chuck turned to face it full on. He spoke slowly, in the same tone that the Spider Woman had used to the four men and four women. "Of course you know that Taiowa is your father. Who is your mother?" Ron said nothing, but motioned with his eyes to the earth surrounding them, just as the first humans had done.

"When the eight did not answer the Spider Woman, she realized that they could not speak. She said to Sótuknang, 'They are all made in the shape of humans. Their skins are different colors. They have life. They can move but they cannot speak. Nor do they have wisdom or the ability to make children.' Sótuknang bestowed these three gifts on each of them, without discrimination, except that their language was different, according to the color of their skin.

"In the First World, in the beginning, the different languages did not cause them any trouble. No matter how much they multiplied, they all felt for each other as one. They could understand each other without language. It was the same for birds and animals as for humans. This was because they all felt and shared the blessings of their mother earth, and because they revered their father, Taiowa.

"But in time, some began to lose their reverence for Taiowa. They forgot the blessings of their mother earth. There appeared the Mochni bird, the Talker. He flew around, talking about the differences between peoples—about the differences in their languages, about their different skin colors, and of course about the differences between people and animals.

"Then the animals began to stay away from men, and men began to separate themselves from each other. Differences in color, differences in language, those who remembered why the Creator made the world and those who didn't . . . differences bred differences, and conflict began to spread until it was terrible.

"Still, there were some who continued to revere their Creator. There were some among every race, speaking every language. Sótuknang told them: 'I have talked with my uncle, Taiowa, and I have come to a decision: I will destroy this world, and I will make a new one, where mankind can start over again. You have been chosen for that purpose.'

" 'Make haste,' Sótuknang said. 'Your *kópavi*, the gateway in your head that connects you with your Creator, will show you your destination. By day you will follow the cloud that your *kópavi* shows you. By night you will follow the star that your *kópavi* shows you. Move with the cloud and the star. The place that they come to rest will be your destination.'

"The unbelievers listened, incredulous. 'Where is this cloud? Where is this star?' They could not see the cloud or the star because their *kópavi* had become completely useless.

"In the end the believers all came together in one place. The color of their skins was different, and they spoke different languages, but they were one because their *kópavi* had shown each of them the cloud and the star and had guided them there. When the last of them had found their way to the chosen place, Sótuknang spoke to them: 'Everyone I have selected to escape the destruction of the world is now gathered here. Listen and do what I say.'

"Sótuknang led them to the hill of the Ant People. He ordered the Ant People to make a hole at the top and commanded the believers to go inside. 'You will be safe here. You must stay while I destroy the world around you. While you are here, learn about the way of life of the Ant People. They work hard. During the summer they store provisions for the winter. When it is hot outside, it is cool inside here, and when it is cold outside, it is warm inside. They lead a very harmonious life.'

"With the humans safely inside with the Ant People,

Sótuknang rained fire on the earth until it was destroyed. The craters opened up and the volcanoes erupted. From above and below, the earth was enveloped in flames. Air, earth, and water became a flaming ball. Nothing on the face of the earth was spared, only the chosen ones hiding in its bowels. That was the end of the First World."

Chuck and Ron were no longer beside the giant sandstone rock. They were tramping over the pebble-strewn terrain in the opposite direction to the road, toward the middle of the desert.

"The same thing happened with the Second World. The people emerged from the dwelling of the Ant People into the Second World, but they began to fight, and Sótuknang was forced to destroy the world again. The faithful were saved in the dwelling of the Ant People. They came into the Third World, only to repeat the same foolishness. So now we are living in the Fourth World." Chuck came to a halt and observed the surrounding landscape as if he were showing Ron the Fourth World. Ron followed his eyes.

"I wonder if this world will be destroyed by Sótuknang too. Maybe it will become a big ball of fire."

Chuck nodded. "Perhaps. People always seem to want to fight." Ron realized he was referring to the war—the one that had just started with the Japs, and the one in Europe that was still going on.

"Taiowa must be angry." Chuck motioned to the sun, now well above the horizon, and with a solemn look talked about the name of their tribe. Ron knew it meant 'Peace,' but Chuck was speaking as if to an outsider. "That is why our tribe does not fight, and has not fought for a long, long time." He began walking toward the middle of the desert again, striding boldly as if his kópavi were guiding him.

No word was spoken for a while. Suddenly Ron began to run. The morning breeze was invigorating and it seemed to push him forward naturally. His legs went faster and faster. Just as he broke into a sprint, his legs suddenly collapsed under him and he fell into a hole in the ground. It was about as deep as a fully grown adult, with a kind of ceiling and a deep back like a cave. Chuck caught up and peered anxiously inside. Ron pulled himself together and lightly climbed out.

"That is no ordinary hole: It's an underground sanctuary," Chuck said, still looking inside.

"It's the hole of the Ant People—that's what it is. If the world's going to be destroyed in a ball of fire, I want to hide in here."

"Good," his uncle laughed. "Well, we'd better get back." It was as if the hole were the very center of the desert, their destination. Chuck and Ron retraced their steps back to the road which led to town.

That night Chuck had a dream. It was not a nice one. The world was about to be destroyed. It was natural, with the world, under the sway of the Mochni bird, embroiled in conflict and war. Chuck was not afraid of the impending destruction. He knew that Sótuknang would come to him and instruct him to follow the star and the cloud which his *kópavi* would show him. He knew that he would be led along with people of other colors speaking other languages to the hill of the Ant People, where they would take refuge, waiting for the destruction to pass. He felt, as he had told Ron when they walked together that morning, that there was nothing to worry about.

Sótuknang left them inside the hill with the Ant People, telling them to prepare for the next world. The people aboveground were going about their daily lives as usual. Straining their ears, Chuck and the others could hear various sounds, like the distant murmur of the sea washing its shores. No, stronger than that—more like the indistinguishable hum of a big city. (Chuck had heard that hum from the top of a skyscraper in New York City.) Of course the clamorous sounds of war, of artillery and gunfire, vibrated through the earth, too, but occasionally, perhaps because of a change in the wind, they could also hear more homey noises like the clatter of plates or a pot simmering, as if breakfast were being prepared. Whenever they heard those sounds, Chuck and the little man sitting next to him looked at each other. He didn't know where the other man came from. They had the same color skin, although neither understood a word of what the other was saying. Still, subconsciously, they comprehended: Their reverence for their Creator created a bond between them. There were two things they wanted to say to each other. Was it somehow possible to save those left outside? And . . . but no, they were being destroyed by their own foolishness.

After squatting down for several hours in the bottom of the hill, Chuck noticed that the clamor of gunfire had receded and the sounds of clattering plates and pots simmering over the range had become more distinct. The buzz of people talking, babies crying, roosters crowing, and especially the joyful laughter of young girls gradually calmed the hearts of everyone in the anthill. The small man's face, which had been stiff until then in an effort to conceal his apprehension, suddenly softened. He offered a faint smile. Chuck felt his own face relax, too, and he smiled back. He noticed for the first time a boy about Ron's age sitting beside the man. Through their wordless bond Chuck understood that the boy was the man's nephew. The boy smiled shyly when he noticed Chuck looking at him.

Chuck nudged Ron forward to show that he also had a

nephew about the same age. Ron frowned but, catching Chuck's eyes, realized what he wanted. He turned to the boy and greeted him in English. To their surprise, the boy understood. "Good morning," he responded. His accent was not refined, but it was English just the same.

They started up a conversation. It was simple, as the boy's knowledge of English was limited. But everyone in the anthill had something in common, which facilitated relations. Ron pointed at Chuck and said "My uncle," then snickered. The boy pointed to his uncle and said the same thing, also trying to stifle his laughter.

Somehow the two reached a tacit understanding to go and see what was happening aboveground. It dawned on Chuck later that Huey, the trapper, must have had something to do with it. Chuck got up to relieve himself, and when he came back, there was no sign of either of the boys. The small man was still crouching there, oblivious to the gravity of the situation. He sensed the alarm in Chuck's voice, though, when he demanded, "Where are they, the two boys?" He rose to his feet, looking very worried.

Chuck read from his expression that he had been dozing while the two boys were whispering next to him and, thinking that they weren't going far, paid little attention when they left their places. But there was something else in the man's expression. . . . Chuck spun around, and along the line of crouching figures he caught sight of Huey grinning at him. What in the world is he doing here? a voice cried inside Chuck.

Huey made a living trapping coyotes and foxes in the desert. He had a thin face with a sly look that Chuck distrusted. Chuck once caught him stealing a coyote from his trap. He was caught red-handed, but instead of apologizing, he had snapped accusingly, "It's because of you Indians that we can't get coyotes anymore."

How could someone like that have been chosen to escape the calamity? There must have been a mistake. He must have told Ron and the boy that it was all right for them to go and have a quick look at what was happening above. The curious boys must have slipped out while Huey distracted the Ant People guarding the entrance.

"Get out!" Chuck's reaction was drowned out by Huey shouting the same words. But no, that wasn't Huey's voice. Huey had become Craig, the Olympic marathon runner. When Chuck first went to the Olympics it was Craig's second time, and he took Chuck under his wing—the poor Indian boy who hardly knew the cities of the U.S., let alone Europe. Chuck thought of him as a white friend, even a Páhana. The story of the white man Páhana had been passed down in Chuck's tribe along with the story of Creation. Páhana was actually their lost white brother. When their tribe was suffering under the domination of outsiders, abiding by their principles of peace, Páhana appeared and liberated them. So, when Chuck first met Craig, he had considered him a Páhana.

The kindness had completely disappeared the second time. Chuck was no longer the Indian boy running barefoot. He was now by far the better runner. He had a chance of getting a medal. The better he did, the harder it would be for Craig to stay in the limelight—the reason for Craig's hostility. The evening Chuck won the bronze medal (Craig came in about twentieth), Craig seized on a trivial rule he claimed Chuck had broken, and tried to turn the others against him. "Get out!" he shouted.

Then something unexpected happened. The small man jumped up. He must have thought that the shout was directed at him. Before Chuck could stop him, he rushed to the entrance, pushed the guards aside, and climbed out. Chuck watched, bewildered, for a second, then made a dash for the opening, too, but as he was trying to pry the trapdoor open, the guards seized his arms and dragged him down. They looked like dwarfs, but their power was awesome. As he was thinking this, Huey came over and whispered in his ear: "Let him go, he's just a yellow Jap monkey."

Chuck glanced up into the eyes of the Ant People holding him. They were filled with immense sorrow. "Ten more seconds," they said softly, but the words seemed to echo around the entire anthill.

They started to count down. The conspicuous sounds of clattering plates and food cooking turned the seconds into an eternity. Such tranquil noises. Peace is the certainty that the present will exist unchanged in the next moment, thought Chuck.

Through the peaceful, domestic sounds Chuck began to hear people's voices. He strained his ears and picked out the higher-pitched tones of young boys. There was no mistaking it—they belonged to Ron and the boy. Suddenly, Chuck heard them cry in unison: "What's that?" As the word "zero" from the Ant Person reverberated throughout the hole, a searing white light from a chink in the trapdoor sent Chuck and the others cowering to the floor.

A deafening bang and huge tremor followed, shaking the entire anthill. The tremor jolted Chuck from his dream. He was soaked in a cold sweat. He got up quickly and, after wiping himself with a big towel, went next door to Ron's house. It was still dark outside, but his younger sister, Ron's mother, was up. She was standing in front of their humble boxlike wooden shack, breathing in the cool morning air to wake herself up.

"Is Ron all right?" Chuck asked. His sister looked at him, puzzled. "He's sleeping like a log."

Chuck nodded and without another word got into his battered old car and drove off toward Mr. Griggs's drugstore.

As he approached the Greyhound bus stop in the middle of town, he noticed an old Ford truck that he remembered having seen before. He pulled up behind it and saw a young man climb out with a sack under one arm. It was Joe. Will was in the driver's seat. Chuck had heard that he had sold out and was moving to the Florida coast to retire. Will leaned out of the driver's window and shook Joe's hand, then broke the morning quiet as he started up the truck and drove away. Chuck got out of his car and walked toward Joe, who raised his hand in greeting. The two Runners had been introduced to each other by Larry in the Golden Eagle.

"This fella here's been to the Olympics" was Larry's introduction.

"You won a medal or something, didn't you?" Joe said in a rough, familiar tone.

"Yeah, something like that. Long time ago—I've forgotten," Chuck responded in like manner. Joe didn't say anything more, but Chuck had been impressed by his simplicity.

"I'm off to the war," Joe greeted Chuck. Chuck wasn't surprised—two or three others from the town had already been called up—but he was stunned at Joe's next words: "What kind of people are the Japs?" He fixed his eyes on Chuck as if he were one of them. It wasn't a hostile look but one of curiosity. "I'm off to fight the Japs, but I've never even seen one. I was born and raised in the sticks, but you've been around, been to the Olympics, seen a lot of things. I guess you've met some Japs too."

Chuck nodded faintly. There had been Japs at the Olympics—in his marathon races, too—but he couldn't remember much about them. What he did remember, however, was the look on their faces when he passed five or six of them in the Olympic Village. It might have been the Stars and Stripes on his blazer. A white reporter once mistook him for a Jap. He didn't believe Chuck when he shook his head and said he was from the United States. When Chuck said he was an Indian, the man just walked off.

"What kind of people are they?"

"Just like me," Chuck replied. "And like you too. They've got a head, two eyes, a nose, a mouth, two arms, and two legs."

Joe took it all in as if he were hearing something new.

Al's girlfriend at the moment was Susan, Peggy's elder sister. He had met her at a dance at the Golden Eagle. Every Saturday night the far end of the bar was turned into a dance floor, where the town's young men and women danced to a pianola or to records they brought with them. A few middle-aged and elderly regulars joined in sometimes, but the floor really belonged to the young ones, like Susan, Al, and Joe. Most of the music on the pianola was dated tunes, but older folks couldn't keep up with the records the younger ones brought. They kept their distance and complained to each other about how tasteless the music was and how they couldn't understand why anyone would want to dance to it. It was not as lively since some of the boys had been called up, but they still managed to have a good time.

Of course the young people drank, but nowhere near as much as their half-alcoholic elders. The dances didn't bring Larry much money. Still, the healthy sweat and energy exuded on Saturday night provided a welcome change from the smell of alcohol and the regulars hanging around in the bar all day. And although Larry sometimes grumbled to Paul, his helper, he secretly enjoyed those nights; the boys and, even more, the girls bouncing about were fun to watch. They made him feel young again.

The regulars would sit there, too, casting the odd glance at the gymnasts on the dance floor, exchanging the latest gossip about horse sales over their bourbons. Most of them were ranchers whose wives were past such antics. "Damn it, one more time. . . ." "Give them a few years and they'll be old sows too."

The girls were hardly dazzling beauties. Most had freckled faces plastered with thick powder. "How could you dance with an ugly thing like that?" said the bystanders to console themselves, but of course it was just the way their wives had looked when they were young. In little towns in corners of deserts, nothing ever changes and there are no beautiful girls. That was a famous line of the notorious grouch Mr. Griggs. He was a regular, too, and the line was uttered under the influence of several bourbons, but there was more substance to it than most of his grumbling. Truly, nothing seemed to have changed in the town from time immemorial, and no Hollywood queen was ever likely to be born there.

In a town of fifteen hundred people there weren't exactly a lot of girls to choose from, but in their "great metropolis" (Mr. Griggs's expression) there were still a few who could catch the eye, the most obvious being Peggy's sister Susan. Some people thought she was really lovely. A typical example from the drinkers' group was none other than Ken, who had the other drinkers' tongues wagging about his recent purchase of Will's farm. Representative of the dancers' side was of course Al. When Al looked over his partner's shoulder and saw her come in, he knew he just had to dance with her. And within five minutes he had his way.

Half of his friends agreed that she was pretty, and the other half disagreed, but even those who agreed shook their heads when Al started getting close to her. She might be pretty by the town's standards, but she was twenty-five, two years older than Al, and already once married and divorced. If Al had any intention of marriage he was downright foolish. He said he didn't, but the look on his face when he was walking down the street, holding her three-year-old daughter's hand, made them wonder.

Whatever they thought, Al was free to do what he wanted. Joe did try to dissuade him once, but Al told him to mind his own business, and that was that. Joe was angry, but he stuck up for Al in the bar when Larry whispered none-too-quietly, "That drifter—he's bummed around from New York to San Francisco. Wouldn't be surprised if he's slept with darkies. And her—she's from the West Coast. Wouldn't be surprised if she's been with Japs too. They suit each other. Let them do what they want." Before Al could even move, Joe stepped in. "Say that again and I'll break your neck."

Larry was normally good-humored with Al. The one thing he had against Al, though, was that he had been around too much, in particular that he had worked in New York and San Francisco. For Larry those cities filled with Negroes, Jews, Chinamen, Japs, and their white Commie sympathizers didn't belong in the United States. He would be quite happy if an earthquake pushed both of them into the sea.

What Joe didn't like about Susan was that she seemed to have come to her father's town just to look for her next husband. She might just manage it too. It was as if all the men were in heat. A cute face, a little wag of the tail, and they all came running. She hadn't even been divorced for six months; everything was going too well for her. He especially disliked her because it was his friend Al she had bewitched. And it was not proper for a woman to come alone to the dance on Saturday night. She was bound to catch people's eyes with all that makeup and the latest West Coast fashions. Joe hadn't been there himself, but he'd heard that five or six of the guys dropped the girls they were dancing with to dance with her that night. Al obviously had the most success.

"She bakes great pies" was the first thing Al said to Joe about her, as if to ward off any further questions. The annual pie-baking contest was going to be held at the elementary school the following Sunday afternoon. Of course Al never went to such silly things, but he suddenly decided he wanted to go when she said, "Won't you come? I'm going to be in it—I mean, my pie is. You do like pies, don't you?" He foolishly said yes, and landed himself in the pie-eating contest. After the "experts" had judged their pies (there was not one baker or chef among them, only people with nothing better to do with their time—even grouchy Mr. Griggs, for some reason), there was a contest to see who could eat a pie the fastest without using his hands. Al came in third and won himself a big apple pie. He didn't even like pies—apple or strawberry or any kind. He took it back to the room he was renting, gathered all the neighborhood kids, and gave them each a piece.

The next evening a furious Susan appeared on his doorstep (damned if he knew how she had found out where he was living). "That apple pie was one of the extras I baked and donated," she bellowed. Al handled the situation like a pro. He took her angry face between his hands and slowly kissed her. And that was the beginning of the man-woman routine.

When Al said she baked great pies, he was thinking of the expression on her face at the door that time. It was the same expression she had had when she came by herself to the dance at the Golden Eagle, and it captured his heart. It made her look young, like a high school girl, or even an elementary school girl like her sister Peggy, precocious and trying to look grown up with a permanent, gold earrings in pierced ears, and Max Factor lips. It earned her a reputation for being tough, but looks can be deceiving. When she got sulky, Al would run his finger down her back. "Darling," she'd whisper, with reproachful eyes, and snuggle up to him.

Perhaps that was all part of her seductive guile. Anyway, the fact remained that she had married, had a child, divorced, and come back to her parents' place. It may not have been as bad as Larry made out, but still, West Coast people—especially girls—had a reputation, and a divorce didn't help right from the start. Rumor had it that she was the one who left him. Their friends were surprised and her parents angry, since he had been a kind and caring person. It was little wonder that people thought she was "tough." No sooner had she arrived than she got herself a job as a checkout clerk in the supermarket. Her forwardness probably intimidated some of the local men. When they didn't come to her, she went to the Golden Eagle.

"Don't be fooled. They bloom until they're married and have their first kid. Then it's downhill all the way," Larry advised Al one day.

"What about men?" Al shot back.

"Men don't bloom. If they do, it's all the time."

"Then, according to your theory she's blooming and I am too. There you are." Larry, of course, wanted no further part in the conversation. He turned to talk to a rare visitor, Will, who was due to leave within the month. Before settling down in Florida he was going to take a trip around the U.S.

"You going to New York?"

"Well, I'll be careful of earthquakes if I do." As Will opened his mouth to laugh, Larry noticed that one of his front teeth was missing.

"Joe get you with an uppercut?" It was nothing so dramatic. He had knocked his front teeth on a shelf as he was getting up from a chair. "You're getting old," said Larry.

Will nodded. "That's why I'm retiring."

"You just look and see how uppity those niggers are in New York. Go to their town—Harlem—they even have their own theater, and a big hotel. Ask Al about it."

Al had told Larry about the theater and the hotel, but he had only heard of them himself. He was no northern Negro-lover, the type that preaches about equal rights. He had worked in New York for a year—on the subway that went up to Harlem, as a matter of fact—but he never went aboveground to have a look around. He didn't have to go looking to meet Negroes, of course. He had even worked with them, and his conclusion was that good people are good, bad are bad, whatever their color.

Al probably thought the same about the Japs, Larry revealed. Larry's conversation invariably came round to them when he was talking to Will. His line was always the same. He hated the Germans, but even more he hated the vile Japs. Just look at their sneaky attack on Pearl Harbor, how they kill their prisoners, and how they killed the crew of a bomber they shot down over Tokyo: chopped off their heads with swords. His usual conclusion was that the world would never be right until every last one of those yellow monkeys was dead and gone. This time he got sidetracked to the Japs who were left on the West Coast. Was it safe to let them hang around there?

"They're not there anymore," a voice interrupted.

"Where are they?" Larry turned to see Al with a patronizing smirk on his face. "Escaped on submarines, eh?

Gone to join Hirohito's army to come and attack us again?" He didn't really believe his own words, but then again . . . "They're sneaky devils, you know," he said, fixing his round eyes on Al as if he were one of them. "In the last war they were with the Krauts too." (He had been a boy then. With his beady eyes he was determined to find German spies: a patriot through and through.)

"Now wait a minute. The Japs were on our side in the last war," one of the regulars interjected. He stopped short, unsure of himself. "They were, weren't they?" he asked the man next to him, who spluttered in surprise at the question: "Eh?"

"That's right, they were on our side," came a voice from along the counter. Mr. Griggs was sitting there hunched up like an old man. He snorted through his nose. "For proof, there was a Jap in my unit."

"Jap. . . ?" Several heads turned.

His eyes moved slowly from one to the next and he snorted again. "Well, it was actually in the hospital that I got to know him. What was his name? Ta . . . Tajiri, that was it."

"What were Japs doing there? Infiltrators, I'll bet."

"He was wounded on the front line and sent there. Like me. I lost a leg. . . ." He paused for a moment to rattle his artificial leg under the counter. The others pretended not to notice. "He lost his arm—his good one. He worked in a factory and said he'd never be able to work again."

"A Jap soldier?" Larry was having trouble with the idea.

Mr. Griggs lit a cigarette, looked at Larry, and carried on mumbling. "Like I said, he was in my unit. He was an immigrant, like some of the Jews."

"But a Jap—"

"The Japs have gone," Al interrupted. The conversation was back to where it had started. Al cleared his throat. "But they haven't escaped to Japan. We're not stupid enough to let them go back to join Hirohito's army. They've been locked up."

"Locked up? Where?" Mr. Griggs stared at Al accusingly.

"I don't know for sure, but I think they rounded up the ones living in the towns and took them up into the Rockies. They've made some camps for them."

It was Susan who had clued Al in. She had just come back from seeing her former husband about maintenance money. "Our old neighbor, Mr. Nakata, has gone too," she recalled, hanging on to Al's arm with a touch of nostalgia. She paused, then in an about-face said in a low voice, "They say they cut signs in the cornfields showing where our bases are so the Japanese planes could find them. They also say that when some nisei soldiers—nisei means second-generation Japs, Japs born here—when they heard the news of Pearl Harbor, they all shouted 'Banzai!' and set fire to their barracks." There had been a hint of excitement in her eyes. She was older but had always been the one to listen. The stage had been hers and she fully enjoyed it. Al didn't know anything about nisei. So there were Jap soldiers after all, just as Mr. Griggs said, Al thought. Susan's flashing eyes had had a certain touch of discernment—the beauty of a young mother. "It's frightening, isn't it?" she said, putting her head to his chest.

"You don't need to be afraid," he said, caressing her thick blond tresses. Her hair had felt good against his chest.

"There, there. Feel better now?" Huey, the trapper, said, raising his right hand to stop Mr. Griggs from saying anything else, and stroking his bearded chin with the other. Two or three people laughed, and that put an end to the subject of the Japs.

Somewhat tired-out, Al took his glass and moved to a table. Will, who had been listening to the talk, took his glass and went over too.

"Mind if I sit down?" He was always very polite.

"Sure," replied Al, not used to such courtesy. They drank in silence for a while, then Will looked at Al.

"Joe says you're going to marry Susan."

"That's what I'm planning."

"When?"

"As soon as possible. Anyway, I'll be going to the war."

"You been called up?"

"No, I'm volunteering. I'll be called up anyway so I might as well volunteer first."

"Are you going to join the Marines?"

"I'd like to, but I'm too old. I guess I'll be in the Army, a plain old soldier. I'm not as lucky as Joe—my eyes wouldn't get me into the Air Corps, like him. But then again, wars are fought and won by plain old soldiers, aren't they? You can drop bombs and send tanks in, but unless plain old soldiers walk in on their own feet, you can't capture enemy territory. Joe likes running; maybe he's suited to hopping around in planes. I'm not a runner, but I can walk." He lightly stamped his feet on the hard oak floor, strewn with oiled sawdust to prevent slipping.

"While he's flying up there in his bomber, I'll be crawling around below, fighting Hitler or Hirohito. You know, I don't think the Japs are yellow monkeys like some of the knuckleheads around here. I don't say kill them because they're yellow monkeys. They're humans, all right. But they're wrong, and they've got to be put right. I might not go to church every Sunday, but I'm a Christian. I don't think people should go around killing each other, but can you just stand by and let Hitlers and Hirohitos take over the world? I'm going to fight because they're trying to kill freedom and democracy. And for Susan and her kid. I'll go to protect them—I'll kill for them." Al sensed the ring of pride in his voice.

"Joe was worried." Will changed the subject.

"About what?"

"About you marrying Susan."

"So what does he want—for me to change my mind?"

"Not that. . . ." Will fumbled. "Anyway, he said you wouldn't listen even if he told you."

"Then it won't make any difference if you tell me or not, will it?"

"No difference at all." They both laughed. Al relaxed a bit and confided to Will that he had once lived with a girl for a while. No one in the town knew about it, not even Susan.

"Where was that?"

"In New York." He took a swig from his glass. "Well, I'm going to marry Susan, so you write and tell Joe to marry her sister, Peggy."

*"Little Peggy?"* Will howled with laughter. Susan often told Al of her sister's secret infatuation.

Al stifled his chortle. "When he comes back from the war with all his medals, that is. She'll be about the right age then."

"Maybe we'd better go and ask Daniel to do the honors," Will said, putting on a serious face. Daniel was the asthmatic preacher. It was in his church that Joe and Peggy had first met.

"Have you heard from him recently?" *Him,* of course, meant Joe. It was six months now since he had been called up. Will shook his head wistfully.

"No news is good news. . . ."

"I wonder if he's on a ship now."

"I doubt it. Like you said, he's in the Air Corps. He's probably still doing flight training at a base somewhere."

"I wonder if he'll be going over Germany, then."

"Who knows. Maybe it'll be the Japs everybody's been talking about."

Mr. Griggs's drugstore was at the end of the main street. A little way beyond, the street joined the highway. When long-distance trucks went past, the second story of his shop, where he lived, shook and shuddered. He was used to it after living there for five years (he had lived nearer the center of town at one point, then moved for more spacious surroundings), but when a line of big trucks and trailers went past in the night he sometimes jumped out of bed, thinking there was an earthquake. A hundred years ago the nearby volcano had erupted, spewing out lava between the town and the desert. It was accompanied by a big earthquake, but Mr. Griggs was about the only person in town who lost any time worrying about earthquakes and eruptions. The others seemed to assume the lava flow had always been there.

When the tremors from the trucks woke him up at night, though, he was more often reminded of the artillery fire from the trenches in France. That was almost thirty years ago, and his memory of it was rather dim in places, but he could vividly remember being hit in the leg with machine-gun fire. As he fell his immediate feeling was a mixture of "I've been hit!" and "Ah, it's over." He felt strangely relieved as he looked up at the sky, then lost consciousness and came to on the rough bed of a field hospital with his right leg cut off below the knee.

Mr. Griggs's dream had been to become a civilian pilot. After he got back from the war he wanted to go straight to flying school and, after that, fly a mail plane. He had fostered such hopes since his boyhood days in this country town, and when he was sent to the front line in France, he would often find himself looking up into the sky, waiting for the planes to appear.

That was when aerial battles were still fought according to the code of chivalry. He didn't often see them because neither side had many planes yet, and they could only fly in favorable weather. But once he did see a French plane shot down by a German fighter. There they were, their wings fluttering above him, like an aerial acrobatics display he had once seen. Crouching in the trench, he watched the pageant with bated breath. Finally the black-winged German fighter closed in on the beige-winged French plane. Black smoke began pouring out of the French plane's engine, and then bright red flames. It lurched, plunged into a nosedive, and crashed to the ground. The spectacle was etched into his memory, minus the sounds of the engines and the stuttering machine-gun fire.

Mr. Griggs knew from experience that once he was jolted by the trucks back to the trenches, he would lie awake until the silent pageant came to him, then he would drift off again. Sometimes in the ensuing sleep he would enter flying school and actually pilot a plane. Strangely, though, it was not one of the civilian multiwings or triplanes he would have flown then, but one of the latest, shining B-something bombers that were now flying to and from their base to the south of town.

Since he was flying a bomber and not a civilian plane, he would be on a bombing mission to some enemy territory. The dream rarely progressed that far, but sometimes he could see black smoke billowing up from the ground beneath him, like the photos of Pearl Harbor in the newspapers. The black smoke came from bombs dropped by his plane, but viewed from above, it looked like black clouds. There was no sound, just as there was no sound in the aerial pageant he had seen years before. There was also black smoke with red flames, like the flames of hell in the book his mother used to show him as a child. In the more recent pageant, though, the elegance and the chivalry were missing, and there was something indescribably ugly about the dream. The flames consumed all sound, including the screams of the people caught in it.

Mr. Griggs didn't think in his dream that he was watching Japan burning. Sometimes his bomber was led to its destination by a large arrow, such as those described by Susan, cut in the cornfields by the Japanese farmers on the West Coast. Those Japanese would now be shut away in some camp in the Rockies. If his mind drifted that far, for some reason it would call up Tajiri, the soldier with him in the field hospital whose right arm had been amputated. Even if he had fought in the United States Army in the First World War, he would still be in one of those internment camps, because he was a Jap. He had been thinking about Tajiri so much recently that in his dreams he would suddenly find Tajiri in the cockpit next to him. It was almost twenty-five years since he had seen him, and he couldn't recall his face; he was just there. He looked at the instruments over Mr. Griggs's shoulder and gave directions: "One mile to target, veer slightly to the right." The directions weren't actually spoken, but Mr. Griggs sensed them. He also sensed the words "Bombs away!" and "Got it—bull's-eye. Target's burning!"

What was the target? What was burning? Tajiri was an American soldier, but he was a Jap. The guiding arrow was made by Jap farmers—maybe it was an American town that was burning. He turned and cried, "Tajiri, you're an American, aren't you?" But Tajiri had no face or voice. No, wait: Tajiri was grinning and whispering in his ear, "That town burning down there is your town, the people in the flames are your people." So real was the whisper that Mr. Griggs's whole body would begin to tremble and he would wake up. He heard the early morning chorus of birds as if they were mocking him.

One morning, after he had awakened from such a dream, his Indian maid, Kate, brought in a letter which the lazy mailboy had dropped beside the mailbox the day before. Mr. Griggs didn't believe in divine providence, but as he tried to make out with his reading glasses the writing smeared on the white envelope, he caught his breath. The name was from the distant past. "Ta-ji-ri," he read aloud, syllable by syllable, as if uttering a spell. For a moment he thought he might conjure up an image of his old comrade, but it didn't work.

The letter was from an unknown town, but he soon figured out that that must be where Tajiri was interned. With a slight tremor in his hands he opened the envelope. One thin page of writing paper fell lightly onto his lap as he propped himself up in bed to read it.

"My dear old comrade Mr. Griggs," the letter began. It recalled how the two had fought in the front lines in France and how they had both been disabled. Then it went on to say that after having sacrificed so much for the United States, and merely for the reason that he had Japanese blood, he had lost his rights as a citizen, including his personal belongings and his freedom. Like him, many in the internment camp were American citizens; half of the camp population was youngsters who had been born in the United States, and of course America was their native country. All this is clearly unconstitutional, the letter continued, a challenge to the traditions of freedom and equality in American society, and quite intolerable. . . .

The letter was written with his remaining left hand and difficult to read, but the gist was clear. It finished with a plea for righteous citizens of America to work to repeal these unlawful acts. "Especially you, Mr. Griggs. You are an old comrade who knows that I fought for my country and gave my right arm for it—you know the value of America's traditions of freedom and equality."

Mr. Griggs slowly put the letter back in the envelope and banged it down on the table beside the bed. Then as if nothing had happened, the righteous citizen who appreciated the traditions of freedom and equality got dressed and went downstairs. Well, what else could he, a solitary person, do?

Kate had already opened the shop, and Daniel Thomas, the minister, was waiting in the worn leather chair.

"Got a bit of a problem with my phlegm again," he said. Daniel was a regular at Mr. Griggs's shop, having suffered from asthma for a long time, but he also made social visits. Despite Mr. Griggs's reputation of being difficult to get along with, the two got on well together. Mr. Griggs was much older; Daniel was only in his mid-thirties, but the ministry seemed to lend years in the appearance of dignity and discretion, and Mr. Griggs treated him as if he were an equal. He usually sat quietly as Daniel talked, contributing the occasional "Hm" or "Aha." Today, too, Daniel started out on the current talk of the town, including the good news of how he had recently joined Al and Susan in marriage, and the sad news that Will had handed over the ranch to Ken and left for Florida. Oh, and the latest news—two more young men had been called up.

"Are you going to the war?" Mr. Griggs's deep voice suddenly interrupted. Daniel looked bemused. As he considered his reply, Mr. Griggs recalled a story about an Army chaplain he had met on the front line. The chaplain was assailed by a soldier one day: "It says in the Bible; 'Thou shalt not kill.' How can you bless us when we're going out to kill people?" Mr. Griggs sniffed, still not feeling his proper self.

Daniel looked dubious, not so much at what the older man was saying but at his motivation for bringing the subject up. Then he smiled faintly and replied, "But we can't stand by and just watch the wicked become powerful. The most important thing for human beings is justice."

It was doubtful that the answer satisfied Mr. Griggs, but the two sat facing each other in silence for a while. Then from the back entrance of the shop they heard Kate's cheery greeting: "Morning, Chuck."

Although they couldn't see him, they could imagine the big empty shell of the former Olympic runner. "He's bringing some herbs," Mr. Griggs said. "There are a lot of them growing where they live." He motioned with his eyes to the shelf where his herbs were kept. Elderberry, sage, wild rosebuds . . . in white bags marked with what looked like a child's writing. Maybe Kate had written the names.

"They'll have to move from there soon," Daniel said. Mr. Griggs raised his eyebrows. "That was originally a military training ground. They moved there without asking anyone—illegally, you know. Their children aren't going to school. They should be back at the reservation." Daniel stood up to deliver his final word. "They'll be using that place as a military training ground again. It's wartime, after all."

The word *war* conjured up an image in Mr. Griggs's mind. It was definitely Tajiri, but his outline was fuzzy.

That afternoon Chuck had a strange feeling. He couldn't put his finger on what it was, but it was bad. He had been down with a cold since morning, and as he lay in bed thinking, something suddenly roused his languid body as if it had been whipped. He put on his boots and clattered down the ladder-like stairs.

He got into his car, which he had been intending to sell to the scrap dealer, and drove out into the middle of the desert. When he arrived at the hole that Ron had fallen into that New Year's Day, he found, as he had half expected, someone already there. A man was crouching, peering intently into the hole. He had a ladder and was just about to go in. Chuck stopped the car and rushed over to him.

"What are you doing here?" the man said angrily, straightening up to face Chuck. There was a bulge in his trouser pocket, probably a pistol, and his hand started moving toward it.

"How are you today, Huey?" Chuck held out his hand. The trapper scowled at him, but his hand stopped and then moved reluctantly to take Chuck's. White man and Indian shook hands in the middle of the desert. The late afternoon sun cast their shadows on the brown earth as if imprinting the image on a film.

"This your new home?" Huey said brusquely.

"No," Chuck replied in the same tone, combing his wild hair into place with his fingers.

Huey pointed to the west, where Chuck had just come from and where the sun was now slowly sinking. "You're going to be thrown out of your place there soon. You plan to come and live in this hole then, eh?" Huey was making fun of him. Chuck said nothing. "It won't make any difference. This whole damned place is going to be off limits, thanks to the Army. I feel sorry for you people, but I'm losing my livelihood too." His voice had softened, and his face showed traces of dejection. Years of trapping in the desert had deeply tanned his skin. The wind stirred the limp red hair sticking out from a weather-worn Tyrolean hat.

The desert was designated an artillery practice area. In peacetime they didn't bother bringing the tanks and heavy guns all the way out there; the coyotes and foxes had it to themselves. But with the war, bombers and fighters were continually flying over from the base in the south. And now the desert, too, would finally be used. A yellow rope had been stretched along either side of the road that ran through it, with signs attached at intervals reading ARMY PROPERTY—NO ENTRY. Before they could start using it, though, the Indian squatters would have to be evicted.

"So when are you going to leave?" Huey had the same high-handed tone as the official who had visited awhile back. Then for some reason he took a pack of chewing gum out of his pocket and tried to thrust a piece into Chuck's palm. Chuck took his hand away and Huey, quite unperturbed, put a piece into his own mouth.

"When are you leaving?" he repeated.

"We're not; we're staying," Chuck said emphatically. Huey seemed taken aback.

It was three years since Chuck had left the reservation to the northwest with his kinsmen. Some of the others visited the reservation from time to time under the pretext of going to a ceremony or festival, but even if he was in the area, Chuck never went back to the land, the rivers, and the mountains he had grown up in. On New Year's Day, when he had told the legends of his tribe to Ron, he had made a resolution to stay where they were. When Ron fell into the hole, he understood that this was the underground sanctuary Taiowa had prepared for them.

Before the New Year, Chuck had been undecided because there was no sanctuary, which should form the center of the settlement. With no sanctuary, they were forced to go back to the reservation for rites and festivals. Now Taiowa was telling them to stay. Chuck had quickly come to that conclusion, but he had to make preparations before he could show the sanctuary to his kinsmen. He chose two people to help him. One was Ron, who, however, was still young and unsteady. After much thought he chose Ron's elder brother, George, to be the second helper. George was strong, skilled at manual work, and had what was most essential for this sacred task: a good and honest heart. The three of them worked at it bit by bit. More difficult than the work was the secrecy Chuck wanted before the unveiling. After working through the summer and autumn they had almost finished, and the indispensable bird-feather *paho* had been placed deep inside the altar. In a few days Chuck was to gather all his kinsmen at sunrise and, with Taiowa behind him, announce, "This is our altar!" Ron was to respond with the cry, "We of the Gale clan make this desert our home!"

Chuck could not tell Huey that, of course. All he could say was "This is a good place to live."

Huey spat and grunted, "You're right about that. Lots of coyotes and foxes here." His words were tinged with sarcasm. Until Chuck and his kinsmen had moved there, the trappers had the coyotes and foxes to themselves. Chuck and his people started setting their own traps, and before long, allegations were flying about broken traps and stolen catch. What stopped the trappers from having the police throw the Indians out was the fear that Chuck might still be able to make enough fuss to get them thrown out as well.

That was how Chuck read the situation. He also know that they caught far fewer coyotes and foxes than the trappers. And there were some greedy white men who plundered what little they did catch. Huey was one of them. Chuck had caught him red-handed once.

"Got lots of rattlesnakes and lizards round here too." He was referring to the "medicine" made from snakes and lizards that the Indians tried to hawk in town.

"And cows, horses, pigs, sheep," Chuck responded. Both of them were caught on that one. Stock sometimes strayed from the nearby ranches and became half wild; both the trappers and Indians secretly killed and ate them, or sold them off cheaply in other towns.

Huey changed the subject. "I hear Sam Pentewa paid a visit."

Chuck wanted to say "Mind your own business," but instead sighed, "He's gotten old."

It was true. Sam Pentewa was the leader of Chuck's opponents who had thrown him out. In the three-year interval he had aged dramatically. He was only two years Chuck's senior, but he now looked ten or twenty years older.

"He came to tell you to come back, didn't he?" Huey cracked his finger joints, which annoyed Chuck.

"That's right."

"Mr. Seymour came, too, didn't he?" Huey must have heard the story from someone from the reservation trading furs. There was a note of challenge in his voice.

"That's right," Chuck repeated.

Sam had come to propose that they forget about their past disagreements. They were establishing a "government" at the reservation and they wanted Chuck to be in it. Seymour, the reservation missionary, had come along in an advisory capacity. "Now is the time for the great reconciliation," he pronounced dramatically. Seymour was a Northerner, devoted to his religion, solemn, with white hair—not unlike one of the Pilgrim Fathers.

Sam and Chuck's feud had begun with the death of the old chief. Chuck didn't particularly want to succeed him, but he did want to make sure his Gale clan's traditions were upheld. The same went for Sam, leader of the Coyote clan, and soon thereafter, the boyhood friends became rivals. Tempers flared, weapons were brought out by the opposing groups—things, admittedly, got out of hand. Seymour and the reservation nurse, Miss Kelly, came running and stood between the two sides. Chuck still remembered his words; "You, you're soiling the name of your ancestors." Then Miss Kelly's anxious voice: "Isn't your tribe's name Peace?"

That name meant they were forbidden to take up weapons and fight—a tradition passed down through the generations from their ancestors. The Gales and the Coyotes all knew that. Chuck disliked Seymour, an ignorant missionary bent on proselytizing them. An outsider and a white man, he entered their tribal sanctuary and even took flash photos. He and Miss Kelly forcibly took children playing outside to their center. But there was no denying what they had said on that occasion.

"What these people say is true. We cannot take up weapons to fight." Chuck's voice rattled the doors of the houses around the square. But the matter still had to be settled. "Let us draw a line and push each other. My people will push from behind me, and yours from behind you. If you push us back and come over this line, you win, and you will become our chief. But if we cross, I will be the chief of our tribe, because my people's power will have beaten your people's power." Sam listened, arms folded, and nodded.

The match was held two days later. Chuck lost. George, who was immediately behind Chuck, came down with a fever the night before and was still weak, which he had never stopped apologizing for. But that was not the main reason Chuck lost. While he and Sam were locked together, he suddenly felt that the whole contest was futile. There was so much land around them. Why, then, were they fighting over this tiny reservation? These thoughts weakened him, and he was pushed back and back by Sam, although he was by far the larger of the two.

"I have lost," he cried. His next words took both friend and foe by surprise. "I am leaving. Those who want to come with me can come." Clan members on both sides were silent as he continued speaking. "When our ancestors came into the Fourth World, Taiowa told them to travel north, south, east, and west. Are you listening?" He looked around, but the only people who seemed to understand were the victorious, beaming Sam and two or three elders. The Gale clan went north to the end of the world, where they met a big wall and were forced to turn back. The Coyote clan went west, and at the great ocean they, too, had to turn back. When they reached their starting point, they went out again in different directions to the ends of the world, and they returned once more. They returned to their starting point, this very land.

These journeys to the four ends of the world were to wash away the impurities they had brought with them from the former world. Perhaps only his childhood friend understood the deeper meaning of what he was saying, that with new signs of impurity and degradation now appearing at the reservation it was time to start traveling again. Sam smiled weakly. One of these degradations was being committed by their leaders—Sam in particular—who were compromising with the federal government, the government of the people who had stolen their lands, to make an Indian "government." With his experience of white man's society, Chuck was convinced that this so-called government would only be a name, something that was convenient for *them*. He knew that Sam wasn't so naive either, but he wanted to become their representative. Some time ago, together with the leaders of several other tribes, he had been taken to Washington by the officials of the federal government responsible for Indian affairs. There they met with the President for all of five minutes. Chuck still remembered the change in his friend when he came back. Elated, even complacent, he recalled the great affection of the President, white man though he was.

"Where will you go?" Sam asked. The sickly smile had disappeared from his dark face. He was now chief of the tribe.

"I will go east," said Chuck.

Sam gave a calm, dignified nod. "There's a lot of land there. You can grow corn. It's a good place to live." The callousness of that remark became apparent when they tried to break in their new land. Desert was desert. If it wasn't a place for war games, it was a place for coyotes and foxes. "The Army think they own that land, but it was ours first," added Sam, who had always opposed Chuck's emphasis on Indian rights at reservation gatherings.

Chuck bit his lip and muttered, "Wherever we go in this country, the land is ours."

The same Sam had come all the way out with Seymour to entice Chuck back to the reservation. They needed him in their tribal government. Perhaps he wasn't as well known as he used to be, but Chuck was still a hero, even for other tribes, and without him as a front man their tribal government would look pretty miserable. Such was Sam's predicament. But Chuck was not going back, however much they tried to persuade him.

With great ceremony Sam unrolled a "Draft Constitution." He passed it to Chuck as if it were a national secret. Chuck glanced over it and handed it back.

"What do you think?" Sam pressed.

"It's all right."

"So you'll come back?"

"No."

"You'll have to leave here soon, anyway," Seymour

butted in with his Pilgrim Father tone. They had come knowing that Chuck would have to leave, and they had the answer to *his* predicament.

Chuck looked at Seymour and said tartly, "Thank you for reminding us of our ancestors' teachings." Chuck had heard from George that Seymour was now preaching on the reservation. "Your homeland is in danger. Go to the battlefield to defend it." The federal government would begin calling the Indians up soon. Sam's tribal government would no doubt be employed to that end. Perhaps that was its purpose from the beginning.

"It's strange, Uncle. At that time he was saying we should obey the teaching of our ancestors and not take up weapons. Now he's saying we should fight." George was slow and burly, but he was not stupid. (Chuck was always telling him he should go to university, to which George always replied, "When I get the money.") His tone had become very serious. "What happens if I'm called up? What should I do?"

"You should obey the teachings of our ancestors," Chuck had said after thinking for a moment.

"You think you're going to stay, but it won't work." Huey kicked a pebble with his foot as he spoke and looked around. "They're fencing the whole area off. Even if this is your . . ." He looked at Chuck out of the corner of his eye for a reaction and kicked another stone. "altar—it won't help you either." He was gloating, as if he knew what Chuck was trying to hide. His tone changed again. "So what do you do here? Hold secret ceremonies and put curses on us whites?"

"We don't do that. . . ." Chuck was not going to be beaten. "We pray for peace on this earth. And—" he drew a deep breath—"and for the world to change."

"The world to change? Are you for the Japs?"

"I'm not for anyone. I'm talking about the will of the Creator."

"Creator?" Huey looked at him dubiously. Chuck said nothing and raised his face toward Taiowa. It was late in the afternoon, but the rays streaming onto his face were still strong. He looked directly into them.

"And what about you people? It's not going to help your pockets if you get shut out of here." Chuck waited for Huey's reaction. Rumor had it that the local congressman had secured a sizable compensation for the trappers in return for staying off the desert. They said it would cost them their livelihoods, but that wasn't true. There were other places they could set their traps.

"We've been working here for years. You people have only been here two or three. It's going to be tough on us," Huey replied as expected.

"Well, we're staying here for many more years yet," Chuck said, closing the conversation emphatically. They parted, each to his own car. As Chuck started off, he let out a huge sigh, releasing all the pent-up feelings from their encounter. Knowing Huey, he would go around telling everyone about the underground altar. That would bring curious townsfolk around, and maybe the authorities too. If they destroyed the underground altar, it might weaken their resistance. But just Huey knowing about it was enough to defile it. Chuck felt exasperated. He remembered his dream about Huey in the hill of the Ant People, and wondered what that portended for the future.

Tajiri came from the same town in southern California as Nakata. For both of them the war had brought nothing but disaster. Everything they had worked so hard for had been pawned off, and they had been bundled off in a bus to this barbed-wire internment camp. They were nodding acquaintances from the town's Japanese Association meetings. One had owned a large real estate business in the center of town and did a lot of business in the white man's world. The other ran a little live-in drugstore on the outskirts. Their businesses were different, their statuses different, and they came from different parts of Japan. Tajiri was from Yamanashi, near Tokyo, while Nakata, like most of the Japanese immigrants, came from Hiroshima. There was one more major difference: Tajiri was an American citizen, while Nakata, who had emigrated much later, was still Japanese. That interval had seen a shift from Japanese being welcomed as a source of cheap labor to hostility and ostracism. Whenever they had come, and whatever their backgrounds or citizenships, in the internment camp they were "Japs." Even now, Nakata kept his precious photo of the Japanese Emperor and Empress, while Tajiri had lost his right arm fighting for the United States in France. But both had Japanese blood, so they were "Japs."

The same went for Tajiri's son, Susumu, and daughter, Emiko, and Nakata's sons, Henry and Norm. (Nakata's third son, Tommy—or Tomio, as he would now be called—had been sent to Japan to live with Nakata's younger brother.) They were nisei, born in America, American citizens, and hardly able to speak Japanese, but they, too, were now "Japs."

Until that fateful day of Pearl Harbor thrust the "Japs" together, the two families had lived worlds apart from each other. Susumu and Henry, however, were classmates in the commercial college of a neighboring city. On the morning they were to be taken to the internment camp, some sympathetic white neighbors drove the Tajiris to the assembly place outside town. From among the crowd of uncertain faces a voice called out "Hi, Susumu!" Upon reflection, Susumu realized that Henry's greeting was directed not so much toward him but to catch the attention of his younger sister, Emiko. The strategy seemed to work. "That lanky idiot, does he think we're going on a picnic?" Tajiri snapped, but his twelfth-grade daughter looked at him with a sparkle in her eyes.

If Henry was a normal, carefree American youth, seldom given over to pensiveness, his father was like many of the other first-generation Japanese at the camp, reticent and withdrawn. His obsequious hand-rubbing annoyed Tajiri, who found himself muttering like the whites, "Why can't they say what they mean, yes or no. You can never tell what's behind that smile." Even the fanaticism of some first- or second-generation returnees with their *Tenno heika banzai*! *Shinshu fumetsu*!—"Long live the Emperor! Long live the land of the gods!"—was preferable to that.

The Nakatas had brought a picture of the Emperor and Empress with them in the bottom of Kunie's dowry trunk when they emigrated to America (Tajiri heard this through Emiko from Henry), but they didn't worship the portrait like the fanatics. On the other hand, Nakata never called the Emperor "Hirohito" as Tajiri did. In fact, the tight-lipped man never spoke of the Emperor at all. When Tajiri denounced "Hirohito," he nodded impassively, but that did not mean he agreed with Tajiri. When the fanatics came round with their *Tenno heika banzai*! talk, he nodded to them too. Again, Tajiri heard this through Emiko. "He's a real Japanese, isn't he?" she laughed, her own non-Japanese quality showing through.

If the fanatics tried to win Nakata over, they never tried it with Tajiri. When it came to struggles for rights, though, they sometimes found themselves working together. On one such occasion they were pressing for higher wages for their work. On another they were trying to get rid of a tyrannical doctor who treated them with contempt. Still, when Tajiri and Matsunaga, a leader of the fanatics, went to the camp director to submit their protest, he looked at them bemusedly. "In your eyes we're both Japs. But we're not the same. That's why we've both come," Tajiri quipped bitterly.

After hearing the news of Pearl Harbor, Tajiri had felt compelled to join in the fight for democracy against fascism. He patriotically presented himself to a weapons factory to offer to work, but was told, "We don't need any Japs."

"I'm not a Jap. I'm a citizen of the United States of America, just like you. I served in the U.S. Army in the last war. That's how I lost this arm." He held out his artificial arm.

"A Jap is a Jap . . . that's all there is to it," the official replied, shrugging.

"Okay, I'll become a Jap," Tajiri told everyone at the camp. Nakata nodded silently, but Henry looked dubious.

"What will you do?"

"I'll renounce my U.S. citizenship and become a Japanese again. Japan's going to get beaten in the war, and then I'll go back to Japan as a Japanese citizen."

"You'll go back to Japan when it's beaten? What's the point of that?"

"To build a new Japan. To build a real democracy—not like the phony democracy we have here."

Henry still looked skeptical. "What will happen to Hirohito in a democratic Japan?"

"There won't be any Hirohito."

"Who will there be?"

"People."

Tajiri was not surprised to hear that Henry was planning to volunteer for the nisei unit. "I'm going to defend freedom,"

Henry announced, but his words only increased the distance between them. "So you're going to fight Hirohito's army, are you?" Tajiri replied. Henry shook his head. "No, the nisei unit is being sent to Europe."

Tajiri belonged to the "No-No" group. There was a register dubbed the "Loyalty Register" by the Japanese in the camp, designed to separate those who swore allegiance to Japan and those who pledged loyalty to the U.S. Most "No-No"s were those who both rejected the U.S. and refused to deny loyalty to Japan. (Many ultimately remained loyal to Hirohito.) At their particular camp, perhaps because people like Tajiri and the fanatics had established quite a powerful anti-authority movement, there were quite a lot of "No-No"s. But there were a few, like Tajiri, who were "No-No"s because they renounced loyalty both to Japan and to the U.S. Predictably, the Nakatas failed to qualify as "No-No"s on either count. Tajiri's wife, Takiko, chose to be a "No-No," but his children, Susumu and Emiko, did not.

"Unlike you, Daddy, we have no choice but to live here," Emiko said for both of them.

"Well, I guess that's true," Tajiri replied with a shrug. Encouraged, Emiko summoned up all her strength and looked at him.

"I know Henry should come and talk to you about this himself, but we've decided to get married. That's another reason why I have to live here."

The Nakatas' second son, Norm, had chosen to be a "No-No." "You're going to be a loyal Japanese, then, are you?" Tajiri asked when he heard.

"No." Norm shook his head resolutely. "I hate Hirohito, Mr. Tajiri; I don't care about the future democracy of Japan, either, but I'm thinking of Tommy. I can't go to war against my little brother!"

So in the Nakata family, the eldest of the three brothers had applied for the nisei unit, the second, if he remained a "No-No," would end up in jail as a draft dodger, while the third was back in Japan attending school as a *kibei nisei*, or second-generation Japanese who had returned from the U.S. He would become a Japanese now, and not a "Jap."

"How come?" Tajiri asked Nakata. Nakata evaded the question and said instead, "Last night we had a séance. Tommy appeared. He's doing fine." Some of the first-generation Japanese at the camp had been getting into séances. With all other means of communications cut off, they were desperate to know how loved ones back in Japan were faring. Nakata told how Mrs. Sato, the medium, had provided great detail, even mentioning the birthmark on Tommy's back, about which she couldn't possibly have known. There could be no doubt that it was Tommy who had appeared.

Tajiri seized upon a break in Nakata's uncharacteristic monolog. "Yes, but look at the three of them. . . ."

"Well, it is a kind of insurance," Nakata replied, his jaws set.

When Norm came to say goodbye, his father was busy mending the trousers he had torn on a nail at work in camp the previous day. Nakata was good at that sort of thing, maybe better than Kunie. He mended his own trousers, sewed the cuffs, and even did Henry's and Norm's trousers for them.

"Father, Mother"—Norm looked and sounded unusually formal—"I have to leave now." He felt awkward using Japanese on such an occasion, and switched to English: "Take care of yourselves, won't you?"

"You, too, son," Nakata replied in Japanese. Kunie was standing beside him, looking as pale as she had been when

Henry had left. She shed no tears, and was silent.

Henry's departure had been more trying. He had left for the war and perhaps would never come back. Or he might come back like Tajiri. For his part, Henry had been surprisingly cheerful. His new bride, Emiko, smiled and talked about how they were going to set up a home in New York when he came back. Tajiri had listened to their talk in pained silence too. His daughter had grown distant, both physically and mentally. Since about the time Henry had come asking for his daughter's hand in marriage, he appeared drained of all energy.

But Norm was going to prison, so his life was not in danger. He joked to relieve the tension. "I said I was worried about Tommy, but I was afraid for my own skin. At least you don't get killed in jail." He had heard of some young men from an Indian reservation who had refused the draft and were also going to jail. "Their tribal traditions say they can't fight. I guess that's how the whites got them in the first place. . . ." The police were already at the entrance of the barbed-wire camp, waiting for him and the others who likewise refused to be drafted.

"Well, Dad, take care of yourself. When the war's over, you can go back home and carry on. I'll be back, and Henry too."

"What about Tommy?" Kunie suddenly broke in. Norm's mention of Henry had set Nakata thinking about his eldest son. He appeared to have forgotten about his youngest.

"He'll be back too. After all, I'm going to prison just so I won't kill him," Norm said, consoling her. She, too, was looking much older.

When Norm had gone, Nakata went right back to his sewing. Kunie sat beside him, staring vacantly into space. "I wonder what he's doing now," she said of Tommy again. "When will we be able to see him?"

"It won't be long," Nakata mumbled, still sewing. The news was that things were not going well for Japan. He inferred from this that the war would probably not last much longer. But that would also mean defeat for his motherland. He tried to keep the last thought from his mind. Anyway, the war would soon be over.

"Seems they don't call them elementary schools now. They call them national schools." Nakata had learned that from the *kibei nisei* Sakashita. That meant that Tommy would be in the fifth grade of a national school. He tried to picture him there but found it very difficult. Between himself and Tommy lay a vast ocean, and the war was now spread across it. Tommy was somewhere on the other side; Nakata Tomio, a fifth-grader at a national school.

"I wonder how Hiroshi is." Kunie was referring to Nakata's youngest brother, who was looking after Tommy. Hiroshi was a dentist. When he was at dental school in Osaka, Nakata had taken care of his school fees. He had agreed to look after Tommy in return, although he wasn't very happy with the arrangement.

Nakata tried to picture Hiroshi, but that wasn't easy either. They had met when he and Kunie returned to Japan to hand Tommy over, their first trip back in over thirty years. The three of them arrived in the port of Kobe after a three-week voyage, to be greeted by a shabbily dressed, pale-looking man wearing a felt hat. That was Hiroshi. Small, with rounded shoulders and bandy legs, he looked rather like the "Japs" in American newspaper cartoons. Apart from his straight back, though, Nakata was very similar in appearance to his brother. Hiroshi bowed, and Nakata had to check himself from extending his hand. His brother looked tense, but a smile of relief came over his sallow face when Nakata greeted him in Japanese.

They took the night train to a country town about an hour north of Hiroshima, near where Nakata had been born and where Hiroshi now had his practice. Throughout the journey, and even upon their arrival at Hiroshi's small clinic, Tommy stared silently at the floor. Within a month his parents would leave for America and he would be left alone. Still, he was the one who had brought up the idea of coming back to Japan.

His father had approved. Having sent his two elder sons to school in America, it would be good to send his youngest son on the *kibei nisei* path—to school in Japan before coming back to the U.S. When the elder sons were Tommy's age, the Nakatas were still struggling to make ends meet. Now they had saved enough for the three of them to make the trip back, albeit third class, in the bowels of the ship. By becoming a *kibei nisei*, Tommy might end up becoming Japanese, but Nakata considered that a possible advantage. If he and his wife stayed on in America, their two eldest sons would be there. If, as Kunie always liked to think (and as he used to say they would, only the urge had weakened over the years), they returned to Japan, they would have their youngest son nearby. Nakata, though, had not forced Tommy into it. It was Tommy who suddenly declared one day, "I want to go to a Japanese school. I hate school here." No doubt his first-grade classmates had been bullying him. And though he never mentioned it, the fact that he was a "Jap" evidently had something to do with it.

Japan, however, promised little better. During the voyage he was in high spirits and became a popular figure on the ship. He began to feel uneasy when he met his future guardian at the "American Quay" and they set out across Kobe. In the space of a few weeks he became morose and sullen, refusing to answer most questions. He found it difficult to fit in with his uncle's six children, who treated him as if he were a parasite. Since he spoke virtually no Japanese, he was scorned by the children in the neighborhood.

For his parents, it had been their grand homecoming. They took Tommy all over, visiting relatives and delivering presents. But always a group of children followed them in the street, calling out, "American, American!" Sometimes they caught the word spy in the chanting. When Tommy was alone, stones accompanied the words. Things came to a head the day before his parents were due to return to America. Tommy came home covered with scratches and bruises. It was obvious he had been in a fight, but he would not talk about it. Clenching his teeth and fighting back his tears, he pleaded, "I want to go back to America."

That was impossible, though, and Tommy knew it. Like his parents, and unlike his brothers, Tommy had a stoical streak—one reason Nakata felt he could leave him with his brother. The following afternoon Tommy went to the station with his uncle's entire family to see his parents off. On the platform he had stayed to one side, refusing to look at the train as it pulled away. Nakata knew he must have been gritting his teeth. He would have done the same thing. He and his wife had spent half their lives gritting their teeth in silence. Nakata was fifteen when he first came to America with a distant relative. He began work immediately on a farm in California, up every morning at five, working straight until sunset. By the age of twenty-eight he had saved enough money to open a butcher shop near Oakland. He chose his bride, eight years younger, on the strength of one photograph, and their eldest son Henry was born two years later. Norm followed, and some years later Tommy, but immediately after Norm's birth, the Depression ruined his butcher's business and he had to revert to seasonal laboring. Past middle age, he found the work exhausting, but in five years they had saved up enough to move south and set up a small drugstore. And then the war broke out.

"What will happen after the war?"

"We'll manage something," Nakata replied, looking at Kunie closely. Her face was becoming wrinkled, and her hair was gray and thin.

"They'll probably say that Japanese aren't allowed to work."

"No they won't. Once the war is over, things will settle down. After they've killed each other, they'll become friends again. Till then, all we can do is be patient."

Patience, and all things will come to an end, he thought, tidying away the trousers he had been mending. That had been his life philosophy. Sometimes, though, he felt angry. Sometimes bitter. Like when he was walking along the street and a white youth came toward him looking the other way. After being bumped, he found himself pushed off the sidewalk and into the street. No, that kind of incident was relatively minor. One of the reasons his butcher shop had failed was that a white who opened up a store nearby put pressure on the city council, complaining about unsanitary conditions and calling for the revocation of his license. The man got an article published in the paper saying: "Jap meat is unhygienic." No, just recently he had to sell his live-in drugstore for next to nothing to a Mr. Chin. (Before the war broke out, Chin used to go around looking for all the world like a Japanese, but had since taken to sporting a badge that read "I am Chinese" in big, showy letters.) So when the war was over, they would have to start from scratch, in which case it would be better to start a new business in a new town.

"How about going to the East Coast? We could try a furniture store there." Having a furniture store had been Nakata's dream for years. A furniture store is more prestigious than a butcher shop or a drugstore. He pictured himself the boss of such a shop, standing beside a large sofa and table, talking to wealthy middle-aged couples. Often, peering into shops in town, he had visualized himself as the prosperous-looking owner. He could envision the sign hung above the entrance of his store, NAKATA AND SONS, INC. Naturally, his three sons, all immaculately dressed, would be inside, ready to wait on customers.

"Do you think Tajiri will go east too?"

"No, it looks like he's going to return to Japan."

"To Japan? What for?" Kunie inquired, but showed little surprise. It was rare for her to be taken aback about things. In fact, she often had a vacant look at moments like these.

"Well, he's so stubborn, and for his stubbornness he'll end up having to go back to Japan."

Before Nakata had time to elaborate, Kunie roused herself, slapped herself on the hip, and declared, "We're really getting lazy. We've hardly had to do anything for our daily bread since we got here!"

It was shortly past noon, and Larry was busy preparing the Golden Eagle for opening time. He had just cleaned the dirty floor with a huge mop and was now wiping the counter. Bob was helping him out instead of Bob's son Paul, who had left for the war. Bob was getting on towards sixty, so it was not surprising that he was slower than Paul, but like his son he spared no pains in his work. (Usually sons are like fathers, and they take over their father's work, but then, war changes such norms, Larry mused.)

"Bob, any news of your boy?" Larry inquired of the white-haired man who was silently washing the glasses. Bob shook his gleaming forehead. There were times when Larry looked at that forehead and wondered how it could be so black, as black as the devil. Suddenly, the door burst open.

"Well, look who's here! What have you been up to, Will?" Larry exclaimed. A smile edged across Will's face as he leaned on the bar and drew some small change out of his pocket.

"Give me a beer, please." He clicked the money down on the now sparkling bar top. His manner seemed affected, not like it used to be. He avoided Larry's suspicious gaze and gulped down the beer. "Nothing like it on a hot day. All I could think of in the car was coming here and having a nice, cool beer." He finally relaxed and looked around. In the far corner on the other side of the dance floor sat the old pianola, flanked by three ancient, dirty sofas. "Hasn't changed," he chuckled.

"Except that the people have gone—the young ones, that is." Larry frowned.

Why? Will was about to ask, but then realized: "Ah, the war."

"Uh-huh." Larry poured himself a glass of beer too.

"Have many gone?"

"Most of them. Some were called up, some volunteered. Well, I guess it's only natural that the young ones should go. I haven't a clue where Al is now, but Joe's still in training. He sent Peggy a card. Would you believe it? That kid acts like she's engaged to him."

"So Joe's still here. He never writes to me."

"But . . ." Larry swallowed his words. How could he? No one knows your address, he thought to himself.

Ken, whose business was thriving, was the first to comment on Will's silence since he retired to Florida. He reckoned that Will must have fallen victim to some evil woman who was squeezing every cent of his ranch money out of him. When an honest man gets taken in, he loses and she wins, he argued. Ken himself had been taking advantage of Al's absence by paying particular attention to Susan. Mr. Griggs later came up with a different explanation. Will must have gotten involved in a business enterprise that failed. Rumors abounded. One way or another, Will had sold his home in Florida and disappeared. So when his former customer appeared at the bar, still sturdy but with his hair turning white and his shoulders more rounded, Larry couldn't conceal his suspicion. Perhaps Will was on the run.

"What are you doing back here?" he finally blurted out.

"I just felt like coming back to have a look. I miss the place." Will looked at Larry and, reading his mind, added, "I haven't run away from anything. I'm working my guts out for honest money, as usual. Not much, mind you." He wiped the froth from round his mouth.

"Working on a ranch again?" Larry had visions of the former rancher reduced to jobbing. Will shook his head. "I'm working in the city." In fact he was working in the state capital. It was not so far away, so it was understandable that he would want to drop by.

"What kind of job have you got?"

"Army work—in an office. Organizing supplies. All kinds of people come to us. I drive a truck too."

A thought flashed through Larry's mind. "Oh, you mean that office?" Awhile back he and Ken had walked past it when they were in the capital on business. It was an unpretentious Spanish-style, two-story building, with paint peeling off the green walls in places. It was built around a small courtyard with access from the road through a small alley. They had gone as far as the courtyard entrance. The place didn't look very busy, just two or three elderly women doing clerical work. They were about to venture farther when a plainclothes cop stopped them. Fortunately, he recognized Ken.

"You know what office that is?" Ken spoke in a low voice, assuming an air of importance when they were back out on the street. "That's the office for a research center where they're designing a secret rocket." According to Ken, the research center was farther north in the mountains. The rocket was nearing completion, and when it was completed they were planning a test flight over the desert. "That's why they evicted those Indians. You know—that runner, Chuck, and his lot." About three months earlier Chuck and his kinsmen had finally been evicted. They had dug their heels in, but were no match for the soldiers, who took them unceremoniously back to the reservation.

"You know how I know about the research center?" Ken continued in his hushed tone. It had been built near Ken's old school in the mountains, away from prying eyes. One of his old classmates had told him about it. Yet another of their classmates, a studious type they sometimes made fun of, had become director of the center. Neither could remember his name.

When Larry mentioned the research center, Will nodded noncommittally. "People are always coming and going from there." He shrugged. Larry remembered the plainclothes guard who had chased them out, but decided to drop the subject.

"Well, it's good you found a decent job. You can save money and do your bit for the country at the same time."

"I'd like to think so," Will agreed, a touch of pride in his voice. He was encouraged to talk more about his work—about the things he was involved in supplying. The other day the director himself asked him to get a chair that could accommodate someone his size. Will had to ask a furniture shop for a special order. All those little things kept him quite busy.

"Do you supply women too?" Larry joked.

"They're all family men up there. They have enough women," Will replied frostily. Larry grinned and thrust his glass toward Will. "Good for them. May they drop their rocket on Hitler and Hirohito soon. Here's to the rocket . . . and to the women."

"Cheers." Their glasses clinked.

Susan didn't like Laura's eyes. In fact, she wasn't very fond of Laura at all. She had a preconceived image of her as a dirty savage. When she pictured Laura's face, the image of a tattooed Indian appeared (she had no idea whether Indians tattooed their faces or not—Laura's certainly wasn't tattooed—but in her mind, they did), and that was enough to make her look strange. Her facial coloring and features were different from Susan's, but she was actually a pretty girl, who had recently blossomed into a young lady and caught the eyes of many men. She didn't wear "typical" Indian clothes but a one-piece dress, rather like some of the Japanese girls on the West Coast. If there was anything "Indian" about her, it was her long, plaited hair, which hung down her back and swayed to and fro when she walked. Even Susan had to admit that it was quite attractive, and from her experience of many male friends, she knew that Laura's limp gave her an air of helplessness which men found appealing. She would never admit she was jealous, but whenever she saw the Indian girl ten years her junior walking away, braids dancing, she felt her heart—and sometimes her whole body—burning.

It was the look in Laura's eyes that Susan most disliked. They weren't shifty eyes, nor were they malicious. They would just look at her as though she were a piece of sandstone. Susan was tall and slim, and there were columns that shape in the desert—at White Sands, the columns were white as well. Laura's eyes made her feel exactly that, like a pillar of white sandstone. Why do you always stare at me? she wanted to ask, but checked herself. There would have been nothing wrong in asking, but it would have been admitting defeat.

Only recently she was sitting at the table in the kitchen, drinking tea while Laura bustled around—ambled rather, thought Susan—clearing the dishes, when every now and again Laura would stare at her. Susan remembered a book on etiquette she had read once that said a maid shouldn't stare at her mistress. No, it wasn't a book on etiquette; it was a story about a black bellboy who entered a guest's room with the morning tray. The wife was standing there stark naked. He carried the tray toward the table, the husband watching. Just as he was about to set down the tray, the husband bellowed, "You looked! I saw you!" The bellboy dropped the tray in fright. Yes, that was the story, Laura, you cheeky Indian wench!

The tea tasted good. Laura hadn't made it; Susan served herself. She thought drinking tea made her like the English. One summer vacation during her student days she had bought a cheap boat ticket and spent a month in London. Ever since, she had had a passion for tea, and made it herself just as her landlady there had made it. She had even adopted the English practice of adding large amounts of milk and sugar. "Yuck, what's that white sugar water?" Peggy would wrinkle her nose when she saw her sister drinking it.

"If you get to London, you'll be able to drink some wonderful tea," Susan kept telling Al before he left. The prospect didn't seem to excite Al, and besides, it was wartime. It was highly unlikely that they would get good tea. The paper said that food supplies in Britain were in a poor state. People were lucky if they could get a thin, leathery steak once a month. The same article said GIs going to Europe were buying up ladies' stockings and underwear to curry favor with the London girls. But Al did not buy any. He was not sent east, to the London girls, but west, to the Japs. Before reaching their country they had to capture all those tiny islands scattered about the Pacific whose names neither Susan nor any other American—including the GIs who had to fight there—had ever heard of. There was Guadalcanal, Makin, Tarawa . . . they were impossible to pronounce. She did not know which island Al was on now, but she knew he was somewhere in the Pacific. And there were no London girls or white sugary water there.

Al had only written once since leaving the U.S. He had written regularly while in training, but it must have been hard to send letters from where he was now. The one letter that did come was brief:

*This island is just like you see in the movies—sunny sky, white sandy beaches, deep blue sea and green coconut trees. But apart from us sweaty soldiers, there's nothing here but men with cloths around their middles and women with sagging tits. I can hear a loud drone. We've chased the Japs out of here, so it must be one of our planes. They're lucky they can fly around, even back to L.A. sometimes. Maybe Joe's on one of them. But the real war is fought by us soldiers, Susan. We go into the jungles and do the real fighting. Not that there's anything on this island worth fighting over. Susan, send a kiss to a lonely soldier who's tired of seeing women with sagging tits with strange oil on their skin. I love you. Will write again soon.*

That was all, scrawled hurriedly on a single sheet of paper. Perhaps he had just been told the mail was about to leave. In a blank space the words "Kiss here" were written in large smudged letters.

Nothing had come since, but there was news from Joe. It was addressed not to Susan but to Peggy. She had managed to get his address, and he replied. Peggy was in high spirits all day, and thereafter carried the letter around in her purse wherever she went. She would not show anyone its contents, but told them excitedly: "He's flying already—bombers! He's bombing the Japs!"

Susan tried to bring her back down to earth. "I wonder what happened to that Jap boy you used to play with. What was his name? Tommy?"

"Mm," Peggy replied, and promptly went on talking about Joe. He was flying bombers, but he was a gunner. He had shot down some Jap fighters. No one knew if that was actually written in the letter, but that was the story she told.

"Wasn't your brother jailed for draft dodging?" Susan suddenly turned to Laura, her mind having wandered from Al and Joe to Laura's brother. She had heard about him from Huey, but the story was fairly common knowledge by now. It had been more than six months since Chuck and his kin were evicted from the desert and taken back to the reservation. Since then, Susan had spotted Laura's short but stocky older brother two or three times; he must have been doing some laboring work nearby. Then he seemed to disappear altogether, and she heard that he had been imprisoned.

"Why didn't he go and fight?" she pressed Laura. If Al and Joe and hundreds of thousands of other Americans had to go and risk their lives, why shouldn't he? "Was he afraid? Didn't want to risk his neck?" she continued provocatively. As anticipated, Laura's impassive expression stiffened.

"Our ancestors taught us never to go to war."

"That's no excuse." Susan had heard all about this ancestral teaching. That's what Laura's brother tried to argue in court. He was the ringleader of the Indian evaders, according to Huey. "It sounds like those Quakers," Susan said to him. Quakers were allowed to be conscientious objectors because of their teachings. She had heard about such cowards, but there were none around here. Her husband had volunteered to fight. Whatever reasons they might give, in their hearts they must be afraid of dying. They were afraid and had to justify themselves. Why didn't they come right out with it and go to jail—that's what she would tell those selfish Quakers if she met them. She felt exactly the same about the "Indian Quakers."

"Let's be honest: Your brother is afraid to die," she declared. She expected a vehement denial, but Laura's response was calm:

"Well, what about you? Aren't you afraid to die? Aren't you frightened?"

Susan was caught off guard for a moment but countered, "Of course I am. I don't want to die. But we have to stop Hitler and those Japs. Even you must know the terrible things they've done—and are doing. They're trampling all over freedom and democracy. If we don't risk our lives and fight, they'll attack the United States. Let them carry on and before we know it, we'll be their slaves. Slaves to those yellow monkeys. That's why Al and Joe went to fight."

Laura tried to speak. She was not buck-toothed or slant-eyed, but there was definitely something Oriental about her face. Susan glared at her.

"You may be an Indian, but you'd better not go around saying you're not an American. Your uncle says Indians are Indians, but that's not true. When he was in the Olympics, he was a member of the American team. Without an American team, he couldn't have gone. Whoever heard of an Indian team anyway? There's no such country. This is your country—America. If it weren't for America, you'd still be running around naked, living like cannibals. Do you understand, Laura? The United States brought you civilization. It clothed you." If you don't like it, take off your dress and run around naked again, Susan's look said. She wasn't finished yet. She had only seen Chuck two or three times, but he looked like any other seedy, decrepit old Indian. She would never have imagined he had been an Olympic runner if Huey hadn't told her. He also told her that Chuck was telling people at the reservation that they were Indians, not Americans. She resented that. They were given their reservation, schools, hospitals, everything—and then they had the gall to talk like that. What was it Huey had said—that a couple of years ago a law had been passed giving Indians practically the same citizenship rights as white people? She wasn't the only one who hadn't known about this law. Very few Americans did. Larry overheard Huey telling her about it in the Golden Eagle.

"What! That puts them above niggers," he exclaimed, casting a sideways glance at Bob, who was absorbed in dishwashing. "Next thing you know, we'll be having Indian senators! Headhunting senators! What's happening to this country?"

Still glowering at Laura, Susan continued her barrage, asserting that rights also entailed certain "duties." Most Negroes and Mexican-Americans didn't understand this, either, but some did.

"Do you know Paul at the Golden Eagle?" Laura shrugged noncommittally. Just like a Jap, Susan thought. "Do you know Bob, the old Negro who's working there now? His son's called Paul. He used to work at the Golden Eagle. His father's taken his place." Again Laura shrugged and Susan felt a sudden urge to slap those puffed-up cheeks. She restrained herself and lit a cigarette.

"He's a Negro, but he volunteered for the Navy." Like Al, he had not waited to be called up. He went to the recruiting office in the center of town and enlisted. He told Susan as he cleaned her table at the Golden Eagle that he had chosen the Navy because he wanted to go on a battleship. Al had been with her then. Perhaps he mentioned it because he had heard that Al was thinking about signing up. And perhaps Al finally signed up because of what Paul had said. After Paul had left the table she heard Al say under his breath, "Even the niggers are signing up."

"Congratulations," Susan said to Paul across the counter when she heard that he had been accepted.

"Thanks. I'll do my best," he answered without interrupting his washing.

"You've got to kill lots of Japs."

"Leave it to me." Paul's big black head nodded confidently. His white teeth gleamed across the middle of his face.

Susan turned to Laura again after several puffs of her cigarette, "What's the name of your brother—the one who's in jail?"

"George."

"George is a coward, afraid of the Japs," she said, letting out the last of her pent-up anger and resentment. She stood up, took the car keys from the table, and made to leave. Laura blocked her way. Although she was much shorter than Susan, she suddenly seemed tall and imposing.

"What do you think you're doing?" Susan demanded. "Get out of the way."

"Don't go."

"What do you mean, 'Don't go'? Don't go where?"

"Just don't go today," Laura repeated, ignoring the

question. Her tone of voice suggested she knew exactly where Susan was going: halfway down the road to the desert, a right turn, and another twenty minutes' drive, to where Ken would be waiting in his car.

"Why?" Susan asked in spite of herself.

"Al is in trouble." Al had appeared to her in dream. He was in pain and seemed to be trying to tell her something. Perhaps something terrible was going to happen to him today. "My dreams are reliable," she said deliberately.

"I'm sure they are. Anyway, I'm going," Susan retorted haughtily. There was no reason she should let anyone tell her what to do, let alone an Indian. Laura shrank back and Susan proceeded on her way, unobstructed. She turned around triumphantly at the door. "If you feel so sorry for Al, get George to go and fight. If he killed some Japs, that might help him." Laura said nothing as she stared sadly after Susan.

In winter as the cold set in and snow settled on the mountaintop, the deer living near the peak descended to the shore of the island and bathed in the ocean. Eul Sun had never seen them bathing herself, but she had a clear picture of them from the stories her grandmother used to tell her when she was a child. She could visualize the deer coming down and frolicking around the water's edge like little children, their wet, chestnut-colored fur gleaming in the brilliant morning sun.

Eul Sun had left her native village when she was only five years old, so she could remember little about it except the rickety homes dotting the gravel road and the deer scampering past. That image was of winter, too—snow capped the central mountain, hoisting the entire island up, it seemed, by its formidable curves—so the deer were probably on their way to the shore, just as her grandmother had said. The winter sea was cold, but it must have been much warmer than the snow on the mountain. Closing her eyes, she tried to picture the scene. She felt the warmth of the water run through her whole body. The fur of the deer glistened, the water sparkled, and in that radiance her heart found respite.

Such moments of peace were linked to her grandmother. Of course they were poor, and poverty eventually forced her family to Japan. But in the midst of that poverty was her grandmother, like the towering mountain in the middle of the island, who had the strength and tenderness to draw the family together and keep them going. Each one in the family seemed happy in spite of their hardships.

Eul Sun was just learning to walk when her father left for Japan. She later learned that they could not meet their inflated repayments to a Japanese usurer. The man's Korean agent said her father would have to go to Japan to work. "He was a Korean, like us," her mother said, shaking her head sadly. "He came with ropes." Go to Japan or die—that had been their choice. Eul Sun's grandmother had resisted strongly: "Leave home and you will lose your heart. Even if you make a fortune, you will never be able to buy your heart back." He went in spite of her protests.

He spent three years as a laborer on a construction site before sending for Eul Sun's mother. Another two years passed before Eul Sun and the other four children joined their parents in Hiroshima. They lived in a single room in crude barracks by the riverbank, along with other Koreans who had suffered the same fate. Although her father had finally left the construction site and managed to reunite his family, they were just as badly off in their barracks as they had been on the island. One thing they did have, though, was a weak forty-watt light, which dropped through a hole in the ceiling near the plywood wall that separated them from their neighbors, and running water. There was only one tap for some thirty families, however, and fights often broke out around it.

Father was still working as a laborer, leaving home before sunrise every morning and coming back late at night. Mother worked in a nearby rubber factory. Fatigue on both sides led to arguments, and almost every night father would beat mother, something which had never happened on the island. Mother for her part always stood up to him. She would seize his arm and leave tooth marks on it. (Eul Sun remembered the men on the island talking of the strength of the local women, and how different they were from the women on the mainland just across the strait. Judging from her grandmother and mother—and even herself—they weren't far from the truth.)

The five children, too, had soon started working: the four boys as laborers and factory workers, with ten-year old Eul Sun looking after the house and baby-sitting for a Japanese family. Every morning, after seeing the rest of the family off and cleaning up, she would set out on the ten-minute walk to the factory manager's house. At first she was supposed to live there and go to school in the daytime, but she got homesick, and the other maids complained about having to sleep with a Korean girl who smelled of garlic. So she got permission to commute from her own home. There was no point in going to school, as her Japanese was not up to it, so she ended up working at the house all day.

She was in charge of a baby girl about one year old, who, for some reason, took an instant dislike to her. As soon as she appeared, the baby would burst out crying. Eul Sun would take the fretful baby—Kyoko was her name—to the nearby shrine compound or the square which doubled as a lumberyard. When the other girls with their charges saw her coming they hissed, "Korean, smelly Korean." No doubt she was rather smelly, more as a result of living in barracks with insufficient water than from eating too much garlic. The public bath cost money and was too far away.

The first Japanese she learned from the other baby sitters was "*Aho! Baka!*" ("Fool! Idiot!") One girl pointed to herself and repeated the words. Thinking the words meant *self*, Eul Sun followed her example, raising howls of laughter from the girls. After two or three such incidents she figured out what was happening and became determined not to be taken in again, but the hisses of "Korean, smelly Korean" continued.

It was perhaps the clumsy way she changed Kyoko's diapers that provoked her mistress into sacking her. Her mother was dismayed, but for Eul Sun it was a great relief. Her brother found her an opening at a tangerine-canning factory, and she began work there. The other fifteen or so girls were all Koreans, and about the same age as Eul Sun, probably because they were cheap labor. She worked from the early hours of the morning until late at night, and for her pains received "teardrop pay," to borrow her friend Pok Cha's expression. During the season they canned tangerines, and in the off-season they made juice. Year round they did scrubbing and washing, which meant fungal infections in summer, and frostbite and chapping in winter.

In time, Eul Sun's health gave out and she was forced to stay at home. It was then that one of the neighbors proposed a marriage partner for her, a man ten years her senior. She felt obliged to meet the man, since at home she was an extra mouth to feed (or that was what she sensed from her mother). He lived nearby, also in barracks. Plucking up courage, Eul Sun went to visit him. The man who answered the door was in fact thirty-five—eighteen years her senior—and looked much older still.

Lee Yeung Sun was not very talkative but Eul Sun managed to learn that he had been forced to come over and work in a coal mine in Kyushu. When she told him of her "teardrop pay" he sighed and said, "I was asked if I wanted the long or the short." *Long* meant the sword, *short* meant a knife. That was the choice his boss gave him if he kept asking for his pay. Thus the five hundred Korean miners were abused by the Japanese. Even deadlier were the accidents. The shafts frequently caved in and in Yeung Sun's fifth year a dam burst and flooded the mine, sweeping more than twenty Koreans, many from his native village, to an agonizing death. From then on Yeung Sun began contemplating escape.

Eul Sun could not imagine how he had evaded the overseers and come as far as Hiroshima, but his nightmares testified to the horrors of life on the run. After they married, he found work as a longshoreman at Ujina, but would suddenly disappear for two or three days, claiming he had seen one of his pursuers. She had heard of his problem with alcohol, and married him only after he promised to stop drinking. Six months later, though, he started drinking again, and just as her drunken father had set on her mother for the slightest provocation, he started beating her. Despite the baby now inside her, Eul Sun, too, fought back, leaving tooth marks on his arms.

Five years and two more children later he was still drinking and still beating her. But he was getting weaker. He found his longshoreman's job more and more exhausting, and often stayed away. As their plight became desperate, Eul Sun was forced to return to her first employer and plead for work. He gave her a job in his bearing factory, which meant long periods on her feet, and her fourth pregnancy ended in a miscarriage. She miscarried in the lavatory at work and dragged herself home, only to be greeted by her intoxicated husband complaining that she was late. Accusing her of having been off playing, he started to thrash her. She retaliated as best she could, lunging at him, but instead of standing firm, he crumpled to the floor. Unable to gloat, she knelt down at his side, sobbing like a child.

From that night on Yeung Sun was confined to bed. He coughed up blood, and Eul Sun scraped all their money together to call a doctor. It was as she feared: Her husband had tuberculosis. The doctor told her to give him plenty of nutrition and make him comfortable, which was of course impossible. Their rations were meager, and they had no money to buy food on the black market. Their three children were already hungry, and the entire burden of feeding them fell on her shoulders. Exhausted though she was from the factory work and the work at home that awaited her return, she saw no way out but to walk all the way to the outskirts of town and steal from the fields. Once she was caught. Instead of turning her in, the farmers beat her so severely that she was barely able to stand the next day. She pretended to be a deaf mute, for she knew that if she spoke her attackers would realize she was Korean and beat her even more. She lied to her children that she had fallen over at work, but her husband guessed what had happened.

"You'll have to be smarter than that," he hissed without any hint of sympathy. Had he not been ill, she would have set on him with all her remaining strength. As it was, he looked pitifully frail. With a vacant expression, he whispered weakly, "I won't be around much longer. When I die, take my bones back home."

At that time they were living in a cheap two-room dwelling outside the Korean settlement. Compared with the disorganization of the Korean settlement, things were much stricter in the Japanese town, whether it concerned the neighborhood association or the air-raid drills of the home guard—and doubly so, thought Eul Sun, because they were Koreans. Once the head of the neighborhood association—a weedy, middle-aged ex-tailor—walked into their house with his shoes on and complained that their blackout during a drill was not good enough. Yeung Sun erupted. Though his once wiry body was now little more than skin and bone, he got to his feet, seized the man and bundled him through the door. Eul Sun long remembered the secret pleasure she got from witnessing that scene. Just as she anticipated, the leader's parting salvo was: "You damned Koreans, I'll remember this! Goddamned Korean traitors!"

One day on the platform at the railway station, Eul Sun bumped into Pok Cha, her friend from the tangerine factory who had become like an elder sister to her. Pok Cha was now living with her husband and three children at Miyajimaguchi, about an hour's train ride from Hiroshima. When Eul Sun told her about Yeung Sun's condition and the doctor's orders, Pok Cha invited her to come to Miyajimaguchi, promising she would send her back with fresh fish. Born and bred in Osaka, Pok Cha could not speak Korean very well, but her parents came from the same island as Eul Sun. She used to ask Eul Sun about the island, and Eul Sun had told her about the bathing deer, so she added as an extra enticement, "You can see the deer on Miyajima too." The old sparkle was in her eyes, and Eul Sun could not resist the offer.

Within the week she was on a crowded train headed for Miyajimaguchi. She was, of course, more interested in fresh fish than the deer. On her way back to the station, though, with the fish that Pok Cha had got cheaply from a local fisherman in hand, she was seized by an urge to go over to the island where the deer lived. The mountain on it was small, with none of the majesty of her childhood island, but the green was vivid and lush, creating a beautiful contrast with the deep blue of the channel that stretched before it. It beckoned to her, so soothing and idyllic.

On the island stood one of the most famous shrines in Japan, which Pok Cha had proudly told her about. Eul Sun could see the great red torii rising from the water, but her eyes were fixed on the shoreline. It was now August—the climax of summer—not at all the season according to her grandmother's story but the deer had to be there somewhere. Still, she found herself walking toward the jetty where the small tired ferry was moored.

"Isn't it beautiful? It's just as if the war didn't exist!" an old woman exclaimed, marveling at the view amid the confusion of passengers and luggage on deck. Indeed, the sparkling ripples of the water and the summer hills and sea beyond made war seem very remote. The old woman was on her way from Hiroshima to visit some relatives on the island.

"But really, what on earth is going to happen? We lost honorably on Saipan. That seems like just the other day, but now Ti . . . eh, what was that called? Ti . . ."

The old woman glanced at Eul Sun, but Eul Sun said nothing. A middle-school girl next to them came to her rescue: "Tinian," she said.

"That's right, that's right. Tinian. Now the same thing has happened at Tinian. What on earth will happen?"

With these last words, the girl lost interest, too, and the old woman lapsed into silence. Eul Sun looked toward the approaching island. Already, visions of deer coming from the verdant mountain and frisking around in the water welled up within her. She could clearly see the wet drops on their fur catching the sunlight. . . .

When the ferry arrived and everyone clambered ashore, there were no deer in sight. She wandered up the road, past the inns and souvenir shops, which were mostly shuttered up, and into the shrine precincts. In peacetime there should have been a lot of deer about, but all she saw was one emaciated deer covered with ugly bald patches beside a stone torii. She stood in a corner of the compound, looking out to sea, bitterly disappointed. A voice startled her and, turning round, she saw the old woman from the ferry, as if she had followed Eul Sun there.

"Do you know what happened to the deer? Some evil people have been killing them and selling the meat. Those deer are sacred; they'll be punished." Eul Sun felt uneasy, for the woman had read her thoughts. "Still, they say deer meat is good for lung disease. If you want some, I can get some from my relatives cheap," the woman said, getting closer. "You're Korean, aren't you? I can tell." She opened her toothless mouth and let out a hearty laugh. "I can tell from the smell."

The colors on the island marked the approach of winter. From their deep summer green the leaves on the trees had changed to yellow, then a brilliant red, and then all too quickly they had fallen, leaving behind a dismal gray-green. It was getting colder by the day too. The brilliant summer sun was gone, and after Imperial Rescript Day, celebrated on December 8, an icy wind blew in from the sea.

Even on such days, Keiji was up before dawn, running along the shore road. On a clear day it felt exhilarating. He never stopped to look at the sunrise, but out of the corner of his eye he could see a red tinge over the island to the east, then a glowing red ball thrust up from the horizon. He had never seen such sunrises at home in the middle of Osaka, and they made more bearable the loneliness of his evacuation to his uncle's home, and the ridicule he suffered at school as a city boy and outsider.

Every time he bent down in the entrance of his uncle's house to put on his old, torn canvas training shoes—ones he had got on ration in Osaka—he would pray a moment for that sunrise and a fine day to greet him. But more often, December brought with it a succession of cloudy, rainy days. In the early-morning gloom he would be able to make out the heavy cloud cover, and sometimes a strong wind and cold drizzle lashed his face. Even then he would start along the track, and when he reached the road by the shore, he would begin his early-morning run in earnest.

As he ran, various faces came to mind. There was his uncle's sun-weathered face. "I wonder how long your running will last. Don't strain yourself too much," he laughed. He didn't think his spoiled city-boy nephew would keep at it very long. Then there was his aunt's sallow face, her hair tied up in a bun. "There's a lot of traffic on that road. Don't go hurting yourself and causing trouble for everyone," she cautioned him brusquely. And there were faces from school: his teacher, Mr. Toyama, a third-dan judo expert who took pride in his ears, deformed from hard practice; and the melon-faced Yokokawa, the son of a fisherman who bragged when he went out to sea with his father. When Mr. Toyama introduced Keiji to his new classmates, Yokokawa had blurted out, "Chicken! He ran away from the air raids 'cause he was scared!" Thereafter he took special delight in ridiculing Keiji: "You weakling! What sort of an arm do you call that? Just like a girl's!" Then came the faces of the other classmates who joined in the insults—Kimura, Tadokoro, Yoshida, Suzuyama . . . long faces, round faces, faces with protruding cheekbones. . . . They always appeared while he was running, stubbornly cluttering his mind. He gritted his teeth in the driving rain as he tried to fling them off, one by one.

Ultimately, it was himself he confronted. If he got discouraged now and failed to enter middle school in Hiroshima City, he would have no chance of passing the entrance exam for the military prep school (the elite track for officer candidate school) he had secretly set his heart on. More importantly, as their teacher and reserve sergeant Mr. Toyama always reminded them, they had to prepare themselves to go to the battlefront for His Majesty. For this, they had to build up their strength. Keiji felt acutely his own weakness as everyone in the class looked at him whenever the teacher talked about that. In his first gymnastics class after transferring to the new school, he was severely scolded by Mr. Toyama for not being able to vault over the horse. "What! Even girls can vault over that! How can you die for the Emperor if you can't vault a horse?"

This incident had prompted Yokokawa to start teasing Keiji about his "girl's" arms. Next to Yokokawa's fisherman arms, Keiji's smooth white limbs did indeed look puny. He tried to hide them, but Yokokawa always came and jerked back the sleeve of his uniform, holding Keiji's arm against his own. "Do all boys in Osaka have your arms? How can you win a war with arms like that?" Then he started clapping his hands and singing: "Defeated Again, Eighth Regiment." It was a song deriding the Osaka regiment. Everyone else would join in—even his neighbor Okuyama, who was usually nice to Keiji.

It was Okuyama's face that goaded Keiji on in his four-kilometer run to the next village and back every morning. Yokokawa and the others—he didn't really hate them, but neither did he want to call them classmates—had been nasty from the start. He had learned to handle their faces. What really hurt was that he had thought Okuyama was different. But there he was, gleefully singing with the others, the double-crosser. "Run! Come on, run!" his expression said. "Jump, if you dare." "Throw!"

Run four kilometers every morning and build physical strength. Add to that jumping and throwing practice. Keiji began his morning run with this program in mind, knowing that he had only his willpower to rely on. No, not willpower, but honor. By running as hard as he could, he could eventually purge the faces, even Okuyama's. In the end, all that remained was his own pale, girlish face, the face of the "weakling." "Run, you weakling, run! Even if you fall over and die, run!" he screamed at it.

Sometimes, as he was running, he felt an affinity with the "American Spy." That was what everyone called the nisei; he was never called by his real name, Nakata—Nakata Tomio. It wasn't long before even Keiji had started calling him that. It was the same as his being called "weakling," only in this case he was on the jeering side.

Before coming to his uncle's home, Keiji had stayed with his father's cousin in the mountains of Hiroshima Prefecture. In September, all students living in large urban centers had been forced to evacuate either en masse or to relatives' homes. Keiji didn't like groups and begged his father to let him stay with relatives. His father consented, and thought his cousin's mountain village would be safer than the seaside town where his brother lived. But within a month of Keiji's arrival the cousin fell ill and was unable to look after him, so he had to go to his uncle's house anyway.

From the moment he set foot in the mountain school, Keiji braced himself for the jeers. He was, after all, a city-boy evacuee. He waited, but the jeers did not come. Instead he heard whispers from the class leader, Sekiguchi: "American Spy—look at him." The whispers were obviously not leveled at him but at a boy staring out of the window. But for Sekiguchi's taunts, he would never have noticed him: Hair cropped short, eyes and nose very unobtrusive, he looked for all the world like a

Japanese. If anything, Keiji, the evacuee from the city, looked more foreign. The boy smiled at him in a gesture of friendship toward another newcomer. It was faint, as if he had just remembered how to smile, but Keiji felt flustered and looked away.

"He's a nisei from America. His family lives there. He must still be American," Sekiguchi continued in a low voice, but he did not seem to care if the boy could hear him. The boy for his part must have been accustomed to this treatment, for he merely went back to staring out of the window. Sekiguchi cautioned Keiji: "Be careful. Some say a corporal from the military police came and said he might be a spy. We all call him the American Spy."

Keiji felt close to the American Spy while running because he was now in the same boat. He was the butt of the class's ridicule; every morning he had to muster all his strength to venture through the school gates.

Thanks, too, to the "American Spy," he had escaped with very little bullying in the mountains. He may have been an outsider from Osaka, that useless city that bred nothing but weaklings, home of the regiment that was always defeated in war, but compared to the American Spy from the United States (which, along with England, constituted "the Devil"), he was at least Japanese. He tried his best to behave like one too. To his shame, when Sekiguchi or one of the others warned him to beware of the Spy, he nodded eagerly and sometimes joined in their chorus of insults.

They laughed at the American Spy's strange Japanese pronunciation. Just as Yokokawa would try to imitate the accent of an "Osaka money-grabber" whenever he saw Keiji, Sasa Yoshinobu, the son of a priest (who was himself taunted with cries of "Yoshinobu, Yoshinobu. Hey, Yoshinobu from the temple. Yoshinobu who eats with the dead!"), was quick to take the lead in mimicking the American Spy's accent: "In America, you Japanese, Japanese spy. In Japan, you American, American spy. Oh, how busy you are, American spy." Then they would all join in, and although deep down he felt sorry for the boy, Keiji sensed that he might be next in line, and before he knew it he, too, was imitating the American Spy.

Keiji realized just how nasty they were when the American Spy broke down one day. He was normally very stoical, which made his classmates tease him all the more, but one day tears started streaming down his cheeks. "You Japanese born here don't know what it's like. In America I was called a Jap spy. When I came here to become a real Japanese, I'm an American spy. What am I supposed to do?" he sobbed.

That silenced them for a moment, but they soon started twisting those words around too. Imitating the pronunciation of some Koreans, they jeered, "I Japanese," even though that was not the way he spoke. In spite of himself, Keiji joined in the laughter.

News of the war reached the mountain school by radio. When the Imperial Navy had won a battle, the news was preceded by the "Battleship March." The priest's son told Keiji how he teased the American Spy then: "Hey, American Spy, how do you like losing? Are you going to cry?" Whenever there was a break in normal broadcasting, they would gather around the radio and wait for the Imperial Proclamation. By the time Keiji arrived, they, seldom heard the "Battleship March." Announcements began with the melancholy notes of "Those Who Go to Sea," followed by a report of the honorable loss of a remote Pacific island by the Imperial Army or Navy. No one asked the American Spy how he felt then. Once the pea-brained priest's son blurted out, "You spied—that's why we were beaten!" He didn't get the response he had hoped for. Nobody clapped or joined in, not because they thought he was being stupid, but because "honorable defeats" were too serious a matter to make light of. Everyone was silent.

That was when Saipan and Tinian fell. With the news came stories of women and children throwing themselves to their deaths.

By the time Keiji moved down to the sea, the war in the Philippines was almost over, and the American army had landed in Iwo Jima. Keiji heard a little devil inside him whisper that this, too, would end in "honorable defeat." At school in Osaka the pupils would get together and discuss at great length the course of the war. They pored over maps and placed little flags on the islands the Imperial Army had occupied. They tried to outdo each other with their knowledge of faraway islands like Bougainville, and sometimes they caught the teacher out. "Teacher, don't you know that? How unpatriotic of you!" they said, giggling.

Those days were over. Nobody wanted to talk about the course of the war at the seaside school. They looked for other topics, like cowards who had ran away from big cities. What a thing to do! What weaklings! Pampered sissies, living lives of luxury, ignorant of the tribulations of farmers and fishermen. . . .

Trucks used the road Keiji ran along, and so did carts. The carts were drawn by horses and oxen that left behind them piles of dung on the road. When the dung was dry, it was picked up and taken to be used for fertilizer on the school farm. On his first dung-collecting assignment, Keiji paused before starting to see how the others did it. Suddenly a voice stabbed him in the back—whose it was, he did not know, since he had just arrived at the school—"What's the matter? Horse shit too dirty for your precious hands, eh? We pick it up every day here!"

In class at present they were learning about the Tenpo famine of the 1830's. While peasants were dying of starvation, people in the towns were eating their fill of white rice, Mr. Toyama taught them. The whole class turned to look at Keiji. Their faces said, "Ah, we have one of those city boys who doesn't know hunger right here." Keiji could not face them. He stared out of the window at the large pine tree in the corner of the playground, the sea breeze playing through its branches, and remembered how the American Spy had been gazing out of the window when he first met him.

Keiji was not sure how well off the townspeople were during the Tenpo famine, or about the starving peasants, but he was famished now. His uncle worked for an electric company in Hiroshima City and had only recently been sent to this seaside town, so he had few means of getting extra food. They had to rely mainly on their rations, which were meager in the best of times. Mr. Toyama's words hit a raw nerve, because that very morning Keiji had been taken to task for helping himself in the middle of the night to the rice left in the tub for the following day.

"We don't want people who steal food in this house! Every time you help yourself, there's that much less left for the rest of us. Have you ever thought about that? Do you think it's okay if only your stomach is full?" His aunt usually fussed over trivial things, but this time her words were few and well composed. They struck home hard. Keiji was clearly in the wrong, and hung his head in shame. He had tried desperately to forget, but was reminded of the incident by Mr. Toyama.

This was the second time that he had felt such humiliation recently. The first was when he wrote a composition for class. It was almost the same as one he had written in Osaka—not word for word, but the same story from memory. The gist of the story was this: A woman walked past a group of five or six prisoners of war sitting on a station platform. She looked at them and felt sorry for their plight. Should she have felt sorry for them? No, she should not have. How could the war be won with such feelings? They had to be despised as devils. Keiji wrote it originally as his honest response to an article in the newspaper in Osaka, but he also knew that the teacher would praise him for it. Sure enough, Mr. Tagaya had lavished praise on him: "Sakaguchi has written an excellent story. This is how the Emperor's subjects must fight. . . ." Even then Keiji was angry at himself for playing up to the teacher.

He did not write it the second time for the sake of praise. He knew Mr. Toyama did not like him very much. He simply wanted to show that he had the Japanese spirit too. He was not the city sissy that they thought he was. Somehow he hoped Mr. Toyama would change his mind about him, but Mr. Toyama saw through it all. Luckily there was no time to discuss it in class, but his comments were written in red pencil at the end of the composition: "A good story, but clearly written to win praise. You must change your attitude." Keiji was shattered. He sat at his desk, head hanging dejectedly over his composition.

The following day Keiji left for his morning run earlier than usual, with all the frustration of the previous afternoon still pent up inside. The rain was cold, driven by a bitter wind. He ran defiantly into the elements, and challenging him were the faces of Mr. Toyama, Yokokawa, Okuyama, his uncle, his aunt, and even his lovely cousin Kikuko, whose feminine sweet-sour fragrance pervaded the air whenever she came near. (Her second-floor room had that scent too. When everyone was out, Keiji would go upstairs and slide open the door to her room and smell the fragrance. Gentle Kikuko often interceded for Keiji, but yesterday when he was being scolded by his aunt, she had said nothing. That stung him to the core.) All were taunting him. "Run, you weakling, run! Even if you fall over and die, run!" Running was the only way he was going to stop his challengers from trampling him into the ground.

As he ran, a thought new and so peculiar came to him that it refused to go away. He must have been thinking about the American Spy when he suddenly wondered, what, at that very moment, boys his age in the enemy country on the other side of the Pacific were doing. There must be thin boys like him there too. There must be someone like him running. Yes, he could see a young boy puffing and panting. That boy was the *enemy*. Yes, he was *his enemy*. "Kill him, weakling, kill him!" he shouted at himself, but the boy's face faded and was replaced by Yokokawa. He tried to picture the boy's face again but couldn't. Instead Mr. Toyama, Okuyama, his aunt, and even Kikuko's beautiful face were all around him, goading him on.

Kikuko had a marriage meeting. The man's name was Hashida, a first lieutenant in the army and, at twenty-five, three years older than Kikuko. He was a distant relative of Murayama, the section chief. Three months earlier he had been transferred from the Kyushu Corps to Hiroshima Divisional Headquarters. "He's not just any lieutenant, you know. He's an elite officer from the military academy," the fifty-five-year-old section chief had boasted.

Kikuko listened impassively but imagined a tall, dashing young officer striding along with khaki cloak flowing behind, white-gloved hand raised in brisk reply to the salutes of soldiers he passed. As she and her mother were ushered into Mr. Murayama's drawing room, Kikuko did a quick double-take. Was there not some mistake? The man in the room was broad enough, but was scarcely taller than Kikuko herself, although she was tall for a girl. His face was large and rectangular, and unlike the photograph she had been shown of him at the military academy, he was wearing glasses. Not that it was important, but he was different from her image of him.

Furthermore, he was dressed not in uniform but in a dark navy-blue suit, appropriate for an employee of a small company who was destined for a life of mediocrity. There were several such dull, middle-aged men at the Supplies Control Association where she worked as a member of the Women's Corps. In a few years he might become one of them. And close-cropped hair goes well with an army uniform, but not with a suit. Kikuko was mildly disappointed.

And yet, she did not find him altogether unattractive. Perhaps because he was a first lieutenant—which, Mr. Murayama explained, meant that he had several hundred subordinates (Hiroshima DHQ had him specially transferred from Kyushu because of his leadership qualities, according to Murayama)—or perhaps because of his natural demeanor, he seemed very composed and mature for his age. He could easily have seemed out of place in Mr. Murayama's small western-style drawing room, but he appeared far more comfortable than the restless section chief. This made Kikuko feel relaxed too. When Mrs. Murayama escorted them to what appeared to be the living room and left them to talk together, she felt pleasantly at ease.

He wasn't particularly talkative, but neither was he brooding. He thought for a while, unsure of where to start, then without looking at her directly began telling of his recent visit to Miyajima and the Itsukushima shrine there. He mentioned the island, of course, because he knew that she lived across from it. His sensitivity delighted Kikuko. She told him about her cousin, Keiji, and about his early-morning runs.

"He's not very strong, but he hopes that if he trains hard, he'll be able to enter the military preparatory academy. I suppose it's hard to get in, isn't it?"

Hashida nodded, although he himself had not been to the military preparatory academy. He had entered officer candidate school directly after middle school. Kikuko felt she had said the wrong thing and changed the subject. "I hear your younger brother joined the Navy." She had heard from Mr. Murayama that he applied when the students at his trade school were mobilized. Hashida nodded again.

"He's now an officer candidate. He wants to fly—I guess that will mean a Zero-sen." He paused for a moment. "I guess we're all doing our service. I'm in the Army, but when it comes to dying, it's all the same," he said.

"Are you ready to die?" Kashima, the head of the Control Association, would scream at Kikuko and the other volunteers during their assemblies. Here we go again, the girls would sigh. Kashima, a gas-station owner before the war, had a habit of approaching rather too closely for their liking. "Ready to die? Certainly ready to resist his advances!" Iwata Kyoko, the tomboyish leader of their group, used to retort. There was none of that falseness in Hashida's voice. He simply believed it was all the same, as the Zero fighter pilots his brother was about to join no doubt did too. Kikuko felt her heartbeat quicken. She was being drawn closer to him.

"Things don't seem to be going well for the soldiers on Iwo Jima either." His openness gave her courage to ask about the war. She had long wanted to ask a soldier directly, since reports reaching Japan had not been encouraging. Following Saipan and Tinian the enemy had advanced as far as Iwo Jima, and from the end of last year, beginning with Tokyo, they had begun launching air raids on the mainland itself. Although enemy planes had not been seen over Hiroshima yet, she had already heard the plaintive wail of the air raid sirens more than once. Iwata Kyoko had heard from a friend that the aircraft factory at Akashi had been completely destroyed in an air raid, and several of the students mobilized to work there had been killed.

Kikuko gazed at Hashida, suppressing the question on the tip of her tongue. *What's going to happen to Japan?* He looked at her. "I'll be honest with you. Japan is in a desperate state. We're not in the position we were once in," he said in a single breath, unequivocally, then paused before continuing, "But . . . Japan is going to win." He smiled, and Kikuko returned the smile. She felt a sense of relief, and flushed.

He did not suggest like ready-to-die Kashima (the nickname was coined for him by Iwata Kyoko) that a *kamikaze* (divine wind) would save them as one had during the attempted Mongol invasion. "In the military, too, some say a 'divine wind' will come. I think that's irresponsible. I say we're going to win because we're going to win." The enemy's advance meant that supply lines, the biggest bane for Japan, presented less and less of a problem. By concentrating their resources they would be able to mount a successful counteroffensive. Their strategy was to give a little to take a lot. "So we need you women to protect the home front." He sounded like an army officer addressing a women's meeting, and shook his head at himself. "No, there's no distinction between the home front and the battlefront now. Hiroshima could become a battlefield at any moment."

"It doesn't matter where we die. It's all the same"—the words slipped out of Kikuko's mouth. Later she was surprised at their pompousness and how they were exactly the same as Hashida's words earlier, but they had felt natural at the time. Maybe they were a true expression of her emotions. She felt a rush of blood inside her and was vaguely aware that this was a man she could follow. She also realized, though, that she was talking about his fate. She quickly tried to change the subject. "Could you meet my cousin and tell him about the Army?" But that implied their relationship would continue—ultimately to marriage—and she blushed even more.

"What did you think?" Her mother posed the question three days later. Mr. Murayama was anxious for a reply. Kikuko responded as any daughter might in such a situation.

"What do *you* think, Mother?"

"He seems very nice," she replied, and that appeared to decide the matter.

"He said he would talk to Keiji about the Army," she said, signaling her assent.

"Good. Then, I can reply to Mr. Murayama in the affirmative?"

"What does Daddy think?"

"He said he seems fine."

Kikuko nodded.

I wonder if the ceremony can be held at Itsukushima Shrine, Kikuko pondered as she walked. On the day her mother conveyed the formal reply to Mr. Murayama, she slipped out of the office at lunch-time and went to the far bank of the river to be alone. There was a wonderful road there which had been made, she heard, by piling up sand dredged from the river bed. From the road she could see the dome-shaped roof of the Industrial Promotion Building. She could also see the three-story reinforced concrete building that served as the offices for the Supplies Control Association. The reinforced concrete had attracted much interest when it was built first as a drapery store, and even now the aged construction stood out at the foot of the bridge. It showed signs of age inside, too, but was solid overall. "It could easily take a direct hit from a one-ton bomb," Mr. Murayama claimed. Kikuko commuted there every day.

That would soon be coming to an end. She used to think that doing clerical work in the third-floor office of that old building was pointless with Japan in the midst of war. It would be better if she worked in an aircraft factory. But she was persuaded by Mr. Murayama that her work was important, too, and gradually she began to enjoy it. The men working there—ready-to-die Kashima included—were all middle-aged or over and not very attractive, but they were pleasant people with whom she could feel at ease without the constraints she might have felt had they been younger. Most of the girls were Kikuko's age, also from the Women's Volunteer Corps, so the office was almost like an extension of school, cheerful and relaxed. The atmosphere suited quiet, sensitive Kikuko, and when a cold kept her at home for five days, she could not wait to get back.

When she married she would have to stop working. Tears welled up inside as she stopped in front of the Industrial Promotion Building and looked across at her office. It had been decided that they should wed as soon as possible. They would select a suitable day in June, just three months away, and have the ceremony at a shrine in the city. But, she thought as she looked across the river, why could they not have it at Itsukushima Shrine, where the deer were?

They would live in Hiroshima City. A friend of Mr. Murayama had a small house for rent, which was about to be vacated. In fact, the house was quite close to the office, so perhaps she would be able to visit even after marriage. But she would still have to quit her job. A certain melancholy tempered her excitement about getting married.

A jovial voice brought Kikuko back to herself: "Kiku-chan, a penny for your thoughts." She knew immediately who it was without turning around. "What's all this? Sneaking off by yourself and getting married—that's not fair," Iwata Kyoko chastised her.

Kikuko feigned ignorance. "*Who*'s getting married?"

"Come, now, everyone's heard about it. Your fiancé's a dashing lieutenant. You lucky girl, Kiku-chan." Kikuko blushed and looked down. The gently flowing blue water sparkled as it caught the rays of the midday sun.

The two of them set off upstream, chattering about this and that, although as always it was Kyoko who led the conversation, leaving Kikuko to answer with a yes ("Are you going to live near here?") or a smile ("How many children will you have?"). Soon they reached the point where the two rivers merged, and crossed the bridge leading to their office. A peculiar bridge, it formed a *T* halfway across, with the stem leading to an island in the middle of the river. Upon reaching the stem, Kyoko suddenly changed the subject.

"You can see this bridge very clearly from the air, you know. Someone said it would make an excellent target for a bomber."

"Really?" Kikuko looked surprised. Kyoko nodded proudly. She always had a story she had picked up to tell. Kikuko had one of her own. According to some gossip her mother had overheard, since many of the Japanese living in America were originally from Hiroshima Prefecture, Hiroshima would not be bombed.

"Really?" It was Kyoko's turn to be surprised. She was not an especially attractive girl, but her well-chiseled features gave her face a distinctive expression, and when she was surprised, her large eyes widened and she looked quite charming. Her surprise, though, might have come from the dark youth walking behind them. His dress was not particularly unusual, but they could tell at a glance that he was from Southeast Asia.

"Good day," he greeted them in respectable Japanese.

"Say, where do you think he comes from?" She asked after he had passed. Kikuko thought he might be an Indonesian exchange student, but before she could say as much, Kyoko continued in her knowing manner. "There are people from all over the world here now. Evacuees from Osaka and Tokyo, and Koreans—brought over to work on the railways and mines. There are lots of Koreans in the Army too." All Kikuko could do was nod and smile. "Koreans can be pretty bad, you know. You really have to watch them. . . ."

There was a tiny shrine to the right inside the school gate, a cheerless, box-shaped concrete structure with a Shinto-style roof under a small clump of trees. Inside the half-rusted metal door of the shrine was the official portrait of the Emperor and Empress. Upon entering or leaving the school gate, Tomio and the other middle-school students had to remove their caps, which bore the gold school badge, and give a low bow of respect. Tomio always felt tense, as though someone were watching him from behind. On his fifth day at the sixty-year-old school, he had been reprimanded by the gym teacher for being too perfunctory. It was not intentional; he was in a hurry because his train was late.

"What kind of bow do you call that? Your heart wasn't in that at all! Do it again!" a voice boomed from behind. Tomio stopped in his tracks and looked around to see the towering Mr. Sugioka. "Nakata, you've come back from America, haven't you? You might not understand, but the Imperial Portrait is the most important thing in this school.

Headmasters have committed suicide for failing to rescue it in a fire," he continued in a softer tone.

"Yes, sir," Tomio quavered and bowed again, deeper this time. The incident made a lasting impression, and now he always felt nervous when bowing before the shrine.

Oddly enough, it was there that he most vividly recalled his parents, far away in an internment camp in the Rocky Mountains. Despite what Mr. Sugioka thought, he knew all about the portrait because one used to hang in a large frame on the wall of his parents' bedroom—high up, looking down on them. He was not taught to call it "the Portrait," but he nevertheless soon learned that it was no ordinary photograph. His mother always referred to it in respectful language, and this, and the word for *Emperor*, were the first Japanese words he learned.

"*Nihonjin* are all children of the Emperor," his mother used to say in Japanese. He also remembered, "If you forget the Emperor's benevolence, heaven will punish you."

He naturally associated the word *nihonjin* with the English Jap, and it stirred in him a sense of fear. One of his earliest, most vivid memories was playing with his brother Norm when a horse bolted into the school playground. It was chased in by a gang of white boys.

"Japs!" they shouted. "Let's set fire to the Jap school." It was not a "Jap" school, but quite a few of the children who went were of Japanese descent, including Tomio's two brothers. There were also Chinese and Filipinos there.

"Japs! Japs!" the gang shouted, running around after the horse. Tomio and the others retreated to a corner of the playground and waited what seemed an eternity for them to leave. When they had gone, he wanted to ask what *Jap* meant, but he couldn't. That one word, he sensed, would destroy all his happiness. He looked at Norm, who seemed terrified, too, and felt all the more uneasy.

After the incident, Tomio came to think that *Jap* meant the same as *nihonjin*, the word he had often heard his mother using. He was sitting down with his brothers at the table one day, eating noodles, when his mother suddenly said: "Aren't they delicious? All *nihonjin* love these noodles." Until that moment, Tomio had never associated the word *nihonjin* with himself. Now it sounded unpleasant.

"What's *nihonjin*?" he asked.

"It's us," Henry replied, stealing Norm's words, then he added, "*Nihonjin* means us Japs."

Closing his eyes, Tomio recalled the scene and the feeling as they huddled in the corner of the playground. Time had not eradicated the sense of fear, and the feeling that everything good up to then had been ruined. "Let's set fire to the Jap school!" the white youths had shouted. No, one of them even shouted, "Let's set fire to the Jap houses. Kill the Japs!"

Sometime after that his mother took him to "the Portrait" and explained very gravely: "This is the photograph of the Emperor. All *nihonjin* are children of the Emperor." To be sure that he understood the word for *children* (or because that was the only English she knew), she repeated "Baby . . . baby" as she stared up. A *nihonjin*—a Jap—dressed in military uniform with a large medal on his jacket, and a woman in formal dress with a sash around her shoulder, looked down at them.

"Tommy," his mother continued in her formal tone, "you must worship the Emperor. All *nihonjin* worship the Emperor." Tommy did not know the Japanese word for *worship*, and his mother did not know the English, but she put her hands together and bowed her head. "Good," she said when he followed suit.

Thereafter, Tomio's mother never wasted an opportunity to say how all Japanese are children of the Emperor, but his father seemed uninterested. His face said that he had better things to worry about than the Emperor, and he did not consider himself one of the Emperor's "babies."

"Will the Emperor bring us our food?" he sometimes said in English so the children would understand but his wife would not. She would look bemused and nervous, while father and sons would burst out laughing; it was an American laugh that excluded their mother.

Every now and then "the Portrait" appeared in the Japanese newspaper. Tomio stepped on it once. "What are you doing?" his mother cried. "If you tread on the Portrait, something terrible will happen." She slapped his leg hard with her hand. Just as he cried out, his father came in.

"Stop it!" he bellowed. "What has the Emperor ever done for us? If he had done anything, we'd never have to suffer like this."

Tomio felt relieved. About a month later he begun scribbling on "the Portrait" in the Japanese paper. He drew in a large, inverted V-shaped mustache on the Emperor's face and was just setting to work on the Empress when his father came in. If it had been his mother he would have hidden it under the desk quickly, but he thought his father might actually appreciate his artistry. Instead his father began to beat him. More than the physical pain, he felt an assault against his being, as if he were being pushed into a deep ravine. "What do you think you're doing?" his father growled, still beating him. "What are you doing to the Son of Heaven? Do you call yourself a Japanese?"

Tomio had never heard *Son of Heaven* before, but guessed that it must mean the Emperor. He recovered himself a little, launched out, and pushed his father back. "I'm not a Jap. I'm an American," he screamed in a shrill voice. He meant to say *Japanese*, but the word *Jap* come out. By then all the energy seemed to have gone from his father. He stood there, head hung low, a small deflated Jap.

That scene sometimes came back to Tomio as he bowed his head before the shrine at the school gate. He could see himself in the corner of the room, confronting his father. One was a Japanese of sorts and the other was screaming that he was not. Whatever they were, they were both very far from him now. Now he was a real Japanese, looking down at them and their quarrel.

By the time Tomio entered the middle school, no one called him "American Spy." Some teachers and pupils called him "the American," (as in fact he was, since his change of citizenship had not yet come through), but at this prestigious prefectural school there was little of the ribbing he had gotten in the mountain school to the north. And if someone did tease him, as Sayama had just after he entered the school, he would not take it lying down. He would confront anyone, even a giant the size of Mr. Sugioka. Such was the steadfast confidence he had developed in himself.

The Sayama incident occurred less than two weeks after he had begun commuting to the new school in the city. He was hurrying along the track through the rice paddies to the station one morning when he ran into Sayama and some of his accomplices. Sayama was from his old school and had just started working at a local factory. Tomio had heard that he and his friends who had gone straight to work or on to higher elementary school were picking on the ten or so who had been accepted to middle schools. Besides which, Tomio was the "American Spy." Sayama had not coined the nickname, but he certainly used it the most. As soon as Tomio caught sight of Sayama and the others coming toward him, talking at the top of their voices, he braced himself for what was to follow.

"Hey, American Spy. How are you doing?" Sayama's gambit was predictable.

"I'm fine," Tomio replied, then added, "How about you?"

Sayama was caught off guard for a moment by the unexpected response, but he soon started up again. "Hey, American Spy. Do they teach you English at your new school? You must be glad to be able to study English. Do you speak English every day?"

Arai, son of the local liquor store owner, joined in "I bet there are a lot of spies like you at your school. And what's that on your head?" He jumped up and snatched Tomio's new cap with the school badge pinned to the peak.

"Give it back. You can insult me, but I won't let you insult my school," Tomio hissed. "Some great officers have come from my school. Lots have died in the war. If you insult my school, you insult them too!" It was as though he were possessed by the spirits of those war dead. He reached out and retrieved his cap from the stupefied Arai. *Well, Sayama, Arai—are you going to defile the honor of my school? Are you?* he challenged, imagining that the spirits of the war dead were behind him. *You couldn't go to middle school, could you? So you went off to work. Admit it—you're jealous, aren't you?* He glowered over Sayama. "Now, get out of my way—or else!" Sayama flinched, then stepped back, leaving Tomio to walk pass unhindered.

Entering the elite middle school bestowed strength on him. He was no longer the boy who sat timidly in the corner of the classroom gazing out of the window. When the teacher asked a question, he was the first to answer. When his group was on duty loading and unloading soybeans at the station, he pitched in most eagerly. He raised his voice so loudly when they were practicing military songs that the elderly instructor, Corporal Yoshida, had to raise his own voice so as not to be outsung. "Nakata has the fighting spirit. Take a leaf out of his book," he would say.

Everyone from the third grade up had been mobilized to work at the engine factory at Ujina, and the only ones left at school were the new first-graders and the second-graders. But they, too, were constantly being called out for one job or another. There was the loading and unloading of soybeans from Manchuria, helping the farmers in the rice paddies, and pulling down evacuated houses. Then of course there were the air raids. With preliminary alerts, classes would be canceled, and when the actual air raid alarm sounded, the students were released from school.

The first bombs fell on the city at the end of April. Sirens had sounded in Tomio's village, so he stayed home that day. The next day some of his classmates recalled the earsplitting sound of the bombs as they fell, and how the earth shook as in a great earthquake.

"It won't be long before Hiroshima looks like Osaka and Tokyo," his uncle commented. Tomio flinched. His uncle took good care of him, but Tomio did not like his uncle's callous remarks. He sounded like a bystander, deriving amusement from other people's misfortunes. He made flippant remarks about the air raids which had destroyed half of Tokyo, Osaka, and Nagoya, and when the Navy port and arsenal at Kure were hit in the March 19 air raid, he said casually, "The battleship was knocked on its side and there were corpses everywhere. . . ."

He had heard about the battleship and also how the army considered these raids a prelude to the Americans landing on Okinawa from a military doctor friend. The raids on the bases in Kyushu were an attempt to forestall any counterattack. Sure enough, three days later the Americans landed on Okinawa. Pointing to the article that occupied the entire front page of the newspaper—by now reduced to a single sheet—his uncle commented smugly, "Look at this. Didn't I tell you so?"

"Don't you mind if Japan loses the war?" Tomio challenged his uncle for the first time. He had just come back from the city, where he had bought his service cap and gaiters, ready for school. Supplies were scarce, and the school had only those two items in stock. On the way back he had worn his new cap. It imparted a sense of prestige, which could be detected in the tone of his voice. "Japan has to win," he said emphatically. "If we don't win, we'll all become 'Japs.'" He ignored his uncle's astonished look. "We'll have to put up with those whites who make fun of us and call us 'Japs.' We Japanese—" now he returned his uncle's gaze—"we Japanese must never become 'Japs.'"

"I wonder how everyone is over there," his uncle interrupted. *Over there* meant America, and *everyone* referred to Tomio's parents and brothers. Despite the fact that all links with the enemy country had been severed, his uncle and aunt still showed off the watch and trinkets they had received from Tomio's parents. "Imported from America," they would tell visitors proudly, without saying who they had received them from.

"I've decided, when it comes to those people . . ." (suddenly his family had become "those people") ". . . I've decided not to think about them. They're Japs. I'm Japanese," Tomio replied surlily. His uncle looked at him suspiciously. He could not fathom what was going on inside his nephew's head. The feelings welling up inside Tomio had brought him to the brink of tears. But he must never cry. He was Japanese. If he cried, he would be like one of them—a Jap. Staring fixedly at his brand-new cap on the desk beside him, he stifled his tears.

Yes, it must be him, thought Kim Su Ho, feeling a rush of blood course through his body. An elderly gatekeeper in a soiled, worn-out uniform jumped out from the hut to the side of the entrance whenever a vehicle appeared, and loutishly hurried over to the driver taking short limping steps. If it was a sedan, it would be carrying an important person coming to inspect the production of engines in the munitions factory or using that pretext to be wined, dined, and entertained by the ex-geisha "draftees" in the factory manager's office. The manager's back room was set up with tatami mats, where the "draftees" would change into their geisha costumes to serve the guests. Kim Su Ho (or Kaneoka Makoto, which was his Japanese name) had learned about this from the sergeant he replaced for his week on guard duty at the factory. The scruffy gatekeeper would bow obsequiously as he approached the driver.

Even if it was a truck, there was none of that haughtiness in him that Kim Su Ho remembered so well. The truck drivers were a rough lot. Just after he arrived he had to dash out to break up a fight. They were not going to pay attention to some decrepit guard limping up to their cab window. If he asked them to present their pass, they just waved a piece of paper in front of his nose. They were not so rude to the other gatemen; surely they were picking on him.

Kim Su Ho had first thought he recognized the man awhile back, but he was not able to place the face until five minutes ago. Their paths had crossed briefly two years before in the most bitter encounter of his life. "We'll do with you

Koreans what we like!" The man's shrill voice was indelibly printed on the sergeant's mind. "You think you're a real smart-ass just because you go to school, don't you?" Su Ho had been going to a small, private middle school at night, where students and teachers would gather exhausted at the end of the day in dimly lit classrooms. "You call that a school?" he snorted, and rattled on about real schools that produced real patriots. "What comes out of your 'school'? Only petty pilferers like you!"

The man's name was Tanaka, a common enough name. This particular Tanaka was a police chief. "You goddamned filcher!" He slapped Su Ho across the face; then he started punching him. "Don't you lie to me." Each verbal attack was accompanied by more blows to his cheeks. "If you're going to steal, why not steal something worthwhile? Why not do something big? Or don't you Koreans have any guts?"

Certainly it had been no more than petty pilfering. He stole nuts and bolts from the factory where he worked as an odd-jobber during the day, took them home, and sold them. Everyone did it, and the factory owner must have known. "That's why our wages are so awful," said one of the others.

Su Ho's mistake had been to complain about the difference between his wages and those of the Japanese. "Am I not a citizen too?" he appealed to the office manager. The idea of a Korean coming to complain about his wages was inconceivable to the ruddy-faced man. His initial reaction was one of surprise, and then anger.

The factory owner chose not to fire Su Ho but to report his "crimes" to the police and have them arrest him. The authorities had been promoting better relations with Koreans, and it would not do to sack one just for complaining about his wages. Three policemen suddenly appeared at the tenement house where he had been living with his mother, sister, and two brothers since the death of his father a year before. Seizing some of the nuts and bolts that were lying about the house, they dragged him off in handcuffs with a rope around his waist. Now they had ample excuse to sack him. After a week in jail, he came home to find his letter of dismissal waiting for him.

All that week he had been the butt of Tanaka's abuse. Once a day he was dragged from his cell and questioned. How many nuts and bolts had he stolen? When he stammered for an answer, Tanaka screamed "Don't play ignorant!" and beat him again. The worst beating came when he said that the Japanese workers were also pilfering nuts and bolts. "How dare you insult His Majesty's subjects!" Tanaka shouted, striking him wildly.

"What about me?" Su Ho cried. "I'm one of His Majesty's subjects too. The Emperor says so."

At the mention of the word *Emperor,* Tanaka froze for a moment, then commanded, "Come!" He dragged Su Ho down a staircase and into a judo hall. For a moment Su Ho envisaged himself the object of kicking practice. But Tanaka pushed him toward the photograph of the Emperor and Empress in the front of the hall and ordered him to bow. If you are a loyal subject, you will bow before the photograph. If you don't bow, you are not a loyal subject. Now we'll see which you really are, his gloating tone suggested. Su Ho bowed low, but Tanaka did not give up so easily. "How about the 'Oath of Allegiance of His Majesty's Subjects'?"

Tanaka said he had been in charge of the Korean section at the Hiroshima Police Station, so he must have known Su Ho's background. Even in occupied Korea the people had to recite the Oath, but not where Su Ho had been born and raised in Japan. Unfortunately, he only knew the beginning: "We are all His Majesty's subjects. With loyalty, let us repay His Majesty's benevolence."

"And you call yourself a subject of His Majesty? Tanaka screeched when he stopped. Most of the Koreans flooding into Hiroshima can barely speak Japanese, but at least they can say the Oath! They may be His Majesty's subjects, but you're not! You are a disgrace to the Emperor!" Su Ho looked up at the photograph. The Emperor was dressed in ceremonial wear, arrayed with medals. The Empress was wearing a western dress with a sash. That much he saw before Tanaka set on him again.

"You treacherous Korean upstart." Fortunately, Tanaka was no judo expert. "Killing one or two Korean worms like you would only be for the good of the country. Let me tell you, when I was in the Army in China, I cut off three Chinks' heads!" he screamed.

Now from the small guardhouse in which Kim Su Ho was sitting, he watched Tanaka limping around. At first he couldn't believe it, but now the memory returned to him vividly and he knew he was not mistaken. The beating had puffed up his whole face, though when he was released after two days the swelling had subsided. He was not taken to court because a big racket had been uncovered and several dozen suspects rounded up. They needed his cell space. "Hey, you . . . His Majesty's subject! Don't let me catch you in here again," Tanaka snarled as a parting shot.

As these memories were churning in Su Ho's mind, trouble flared up between Tanaka and a truck driver. Tanaka's face had gone dark red and he was shouting into the cab window in his high-pitched, metallic voice. The cab door swung open and two men in their forties jumped out. Su Ho leaped up and dashed toward the truck. As he was covering the ten-meter distance from the guardhouse, the two men started punching Tanaka. One of them had a wrench in his hand. Su Ho jumped between them and wrested the wrench from the man.

The well-built sergeant could have handled both of them, but he did not need to. He was in uniform. "Fight His Majesty's army, would you?" he challenged them, and they backed off. "Dismissed!" The men climbed back into the truck and drove off.

"Thank you," Tanaka said, recovering his senses. "How can I repay you?"

Su Ho threw the wrench onto a pile of gravel beside the entrance. "You used to be in the police force, didn't you?"

Tanaka looked at him in momentary surprise. He could not imagine that the man standing before him in the Imperial Army uniform, sergeant's insignia glistening on the collar, could be the treacherous Korean pilferer. Su Ho had heard that Tanaka had left—or had been forced to leave—as a result of being caught lining his pockets from the black market.

"Why did you quit?" If I'm a pilferer, what does that make you? Su Ho almost gloated. "What did you do to your leg? You're limping, aren't you?"

Tanaka managed to mumble that he had injured it in a traffic accident. Su Ho regretted that he did not press Tanaka further, for the brief pause allowed him to start berating his assailants.

"What can you do with people like that? They must be Koreans. If they weren't, at their age they'd be in the Army."

Su Ho felt stirred up again—the same as when he first realized the gatekeeper was Tanaka. Instead of finding release, however, the feeling stayed bottled up inside him, a turbulent mixture of anger and shame.

*I'm a Korean too.* The words were biting his tongue but he stifled them, along with his emotions.

He was reminded of Sakura, a girl in the red-light district not far from the factory. At one time he would go to see her whenever he got leave. About all she ever said to please him was "I like soldiers because they are frank." She always limited her conversation to the simplest of responses, just enough to keep the talk flowing, and never spoke of herself.

She wasn't particularly beautiful, but he liked her chubby, round face, and especially her body. Her soft, velvety skin seemed to melt into his, and her suppleness excited him. Many other customers craved her body, too, and he was often kept waiting. One night while he was sitting in the little waiting room, smoking a cigarette, a bald man who introduced himself as the master of the shop came up to him.

"You soldiers are serving the Emperor well, but we are doing our bit here too." He showed Su Ho a certificate of appointment that indicated that he was the head of a small aerial defense detachment. "Whatever happens, we have to win. Please do your best." He paused. "We have some nice girls here, don't we? Take Sakura. Isn't she superb?" He remembered the bald man's words because it was to be the last time he would see Sakura.

About three days later, as he was lounging in the sun in the barrack square, the sergeant in charge of uniforms began to talk about Sakura. He was another of her admirers. Su Ho sat with his back toward him, feigning indifference.

"The girls from your country are different from Japanese girls," he chuckled. *Your country. Japanese girls*. The words stunned Su Ho, not so much because the sergeant knew about him, but at what they said about Sakura. He felt blood rush to his head and a volatile mixture of rage and shame.

"She was brought over from Cheju, you know. If people found out she was Korean she would lose her customers, so they gave her a Japanese name. She can't speak much Japanese. You can see why she never opens her mouth. All she says to us is she likes soldiers because they're frank."

Su Ho finally turned and the sergeant said to him, "Come, Sergeant Kaneoka. We're like brothers in a way: You, too, were silly enough to volunteer for the Army. Let's shake hands for better relations between Japanese and Koreans." He offered his hand with the authority of an old soldier to a new recruit. Su Ho proffered his own hand in silence. The old soldier's hand was strangely soft, and for a moment Su Ho recalled the sensation of Sakura's body.

"Koreans are getting called up these days," Tanaka said, breaking his reverie. "It's about time too. How can you talk about unity if they get off like those two. If they were Japanese, they'd be doing their duty now instead of cavorting about in trucks." Tanaka looked up at the sergeant, seeing only his uniform. "You know what I think? If the Koreans aren't going to join the Army and fight for Japan, they've got no right to complain if they're not treated the same as Japanese. That's what I think."

Su Ho turned his back while Tanaka was in mid-sentence and walked away. *You didn't wait to be drafted with the other Koreans because you wanted to be treated like a Japanese! Why else would you be stupid enough to volunteer for the Imperial Army?* Tanaka's words shot him clean through in the back.

Keiji sat silently in front of his cousin's fiancé. Then, as though having suddenly made up his mind, he said: "I've given up the idea of applying for the military preparatory academy." There was no hint of strength in his gaze. The Lieutenant was not surprised. Keiji had lost both of his parents in an air raid ten days before. Last Saturday night Hashida had come home early and was drinking a beer in the downstairs living room of the two-story house he was renting. He was just thinking that in two months he would be making his home with Kikuko, when the landlord's wife poked her head over the garden fence from next door and called out, "Telephone!" Ten to one it was from Kikuko. He was right. Her somewhat high-pitched voice vibrated through the receiver. But his other guess—that her mother had said something about the list of guests to be invited to the reception—was off the mark. Kikuko was trying to sound calm but he could tell that something was wrong by her slow deliberate tone.

"Keiji's parents died in the air raids over Osaka three days ago. He's just returned. . . . Yes, he was back in Osaka for a while . . . for his grandfather's memorial service, and something to do with his application for military prep school. . . ." Her voice trailed off into sobs.

According to the story she told Hashida later, about half an hour before her phone call they had heard a noise on the porch. Her mother went to look and found Keiji standing in a daze, his face black as soot, with his elder brother, Wataru, next to him. "Auntie, they're dead. Mom and Dad, both dead," he said. Her mother said people in a state of shock act strangely, and there Keiji was grinning like a fool. He told them vacantly how his home had burned to the ground as if it had been someone else's house and family.

It was the first time in a year that he had returned to Osaka. Kikuko and her mother had urged him to go back for the New Year, and then again when he entered middle school in April. "Why don't you go and show your mother your new cap?" they suggested, but he would not budge. His pride equated going home with giving in. Finally his maternal grandfather's memorial service gave him a reason, and his mother wrote numerous letters asking that he return.

"All right, but only for a couple of days," he had consented. He also needed a copy of his family register for his application for the military preparatory academy. Armed with two excuses, and the ticket Kikuko had got him through connections at the Association, he boarded the night train for Osaka.

The next day had been the memorial service and the following day, just as he was about to return, the daytime air raids had begun. Wataru barely managed to escape from the factory he was working in before it was enveloped in flames. Keiji was out visiting relatives in the city and escaped, but could risk returning home only when the sea of flames engulfing the city began to subside. When he arrived, he discovered that their wooden two-story house had been reduced to a pile of charred rubble and smoldering embers.

Among the debris lay two half-buried objects, one on top of the other, charred like the surroundings, but with softer outlines. The chief of the home guard unit was trying to dig them out with a shovel. He looked up at the same instant that Keiji felt a shock, like a lightning bolt through his body. Both of them froze, then the home guard chief, who had run a local store until its enforced closure, stood up stiffly and uttered, "Your parents died an honorable death." He looked clumsy, like the middle-aged men practicing on street corners before being called up. He obviously did not know what to say next, but he suddenly raised both hands and shouted hoarsely three times: "Long live the Emperor!"

The Lieutenant had not heard from the unstirring youth sitting in perfect posture before him now. He had heard the entire story from Kikuko two or three days after her call. "Keiji wants to come and see you soon. He said there was something he has to talk to you about," she had said, looking worried.

Keiji had stubbornly refused to tell her what it was. That was two or three days ago. Now, tonight, when the Lieutenant was returning home close to midnight, he noticed a figure beside the gate.

"Who's there?" he demanded. The shadow moved feebly toward him, as though it were about to fall at his feet.

"It's me: Keiji. I'm staying with the Yamada's." He identified himself using Kikuko's surname. "Can I talk with you?"

Hashida ushered him into the living room, where Keiji sat down stiffly on the tatami-mat flooring, without speaking a word. "Relax, make yourself at home," Hashida said, sitting cross-legged on the mat himself, but the boy did not move. Nor did he make any attempt to take the canned tangerines offered him. Neither spoke, until finally the boy seemed unable to endure the silence.

"I've given up the idea of applying for military prep school," he stammered slightly.

"Why?" The Lieutenant folded his arms and frowned, but there was no answer from the youth. "Do you value your life so much?"

He was sorry for Keiji but, confronted with this silence, he felt a tide of anger. "If life means that much to you, you'd better not join the Army, let alone a school that trains the Army's commanders. You're right. You'd better give up the idea."

He frowned again. Kikuko had told him in their first meeting about her cousin from Osaka, but he had only met the boy after they became officially engaged, when, two or three times, she had brought him along. From behind, his neck looked oddly delicate, like a girl's. Even now, when he was in an elite middle school and sporting a service cap, he looked like a girl dressed up as a soldier. A normal cap might have looked different, but the military-style cap accentuated his effeminate profile. It was hard to believe he was running four kilometers every morning.

"Are you still running?"

"Yes." His voice was unexpectedly strong and clear. It suggested a tenacity that was lacking in some of the recent student soldiers.

"Do you think he can become a good soldier?" Kikuko had once asked her fiancé.

"Yes, I think so. If he gets into military prep school he'll be toughened up." Whether he can take the discipline is up to him, the Lieutenant had thought.

A week or two ago they had talked about one of the nisei in his regiment, born and raised in the United States until his teens. He had a tough time at first: If he did anything wrong, he received twenty blows instead of ten. The squad leader was so severe that the company commander, a friend of the Lieutenant, began to worry about him. Yet, he pulled through, winning first prize in the bayonet competition and becoming one of the first fifteen to be promoted to lance corporal.

Keiji was present and mentioned the nisei in his class in the mountains who was always teased as the "American Spy." Now they were in the same school together, both commuting in by train. The change that had come over him was remarkable. The taunting he had gotten in the mountains had obviously made him tough. When they practiced with their wooden bayonets, he was always the most aggressive. "He can see the American devil," the teacher pointed out, and the nisei youth would glare all the fiercer at the imaginary devil he had just stabbed, cringing before him.

"They used to pick on him in America," said Keiji, trying to sound like an adult. Then he mentioned the American prisoners he had seen at a train station in Osaka. They were squatting on the platform, eating rice balls. Their faces were very sunburned; to him they really did look like devils.

"Are there any prisoners of war in Hiroshima?" he asked.

"Hmm, I wonder," the Lieutenant replied vaguely. He had seen two or three at headquarters, sent up from Kyushu, where they had been shot down on bombing raids. They were walking, handcuffed, in tattered uniforms. Their faces were not sunburned like the ones Keiji had seen, perhaps because they had been imprisoned, but neither were they white; they looked rather ashen, not a bit like "American devils."

That conversation had taken place less than two weeks before. Keiji's world had since turned upside down. Realizing this, the Lieutenant wanted more than anything to sympathize with him, yet somehow, he could not. Kikuko had asked him to talk to the boy because he wanted to hear all about life in the Army. Obliging her, he had recounted his memories, from the time he entered officer candidate school right down to the present. Considering now that it had really all been a waste of effort, the Lieutenant felt irritated. "If life means so much to you . . . " he started again.

"It doesn't," the boy interrupted. "The American devil killed my parents. Why should life mean so much to me?" He looked the Lieutenant in the eyes. He was angry. "It is because life doesn't mean that much to me that I'm not going to the military prep school. If it did, I would go."

The Lieutenant was taken aback. He wanted to respond but gave up, and instead continued to sit with arms folded in silence.

"You've got to be a coward to go to military prep school. That's what I think."

Coward? The Lieutenant suppressed an exclamation and looked at the boy. Keiji looked back, and the Lieutenant felt mildly uncomfortable.

"Everyone's dying," Keiji continued. "At the front and at home. The time has come for all Japanese to take up weapons and fight. There's no time to go to military prep school and then on to the Academy. Of course we need officers, but it takes years to become one, and by then it will be too late. It's all right for people like you who're already officers"—he was lecturing the Lieutenant—"but us little people have to go and fight now. That's why I think it's cowardly to take the exam for the prep school. I'm going to apply for pilot training," he declared, with a ring of challenge to his words.

"Yes, that's also a good idea. You'll be giving everything for your country that way too," the Lieutenant replied in a restrained tone. "Your parents died an honorable death. When it comes to serving the nation, there's no distinction between the battlefront and the home front," he added, expressing his sympathy.

Keiji seemed to be on the verge of speaking. Was there something he wanted to say? the Lieutenant asked, softening his voice and expression. Keiji shook his head, but there was clearly still something on his mind.

"Let's go to sleep. Please stay for the night." The Lieutenant stood up and, after making the necessary preparations, left the boy alone.

Toward dawn the Lieutenant was awakened by a loud groan coming from the next room. He hurriedly slid open the dividing partition. "What's the matter?" he called out. The groaning ceased and the boy woke up.

"I had . . . a dream," he replied groggily.

"A nightmare?"

"I think . . . it was about an air raid. There was a shower of fire coming down from the sky. "

"Where were you?"

"On the ground—charred black."

"Did you die?" The Lieutenant was surprised at his own words.

"Yes, I did."

"Were you afraid?"

"No."

"Well, why did you groan, then?"

The boy looked at the Lieutenant dubiously. "I didn't groan," he said, his expression changing to anger. "I shouted 'Long live the Emperor!' Isn't that what you heard?"

The Lieutenant looked away from the pathetic boy.

"No, it isn't. I heard you groan."

What was that light? Mr. Griggs reacted instantaneously. As usual, he awoke before dawn, but had stayed in this morning to wait for the storm raging outside to subside. He could hear the driving rain on the roof and walls. Now and then light penetrated the edges of the heavy wooden shutters, soon followed by loud peals of thunder. He lay motionless in the dark and, after dozing off again, awoke with a start. He could just make out the time from the antique clock on his bedside table. It read five thirty. Suddenly, every corner of the room lit up, like a magnesium flash from the photographer's camera at Daniel's weddings. It was only momentary, and the room went dark again. The old man jumped out of bed, threw on his robe, and went to the window. Before he could open it a deafening roar, like hundreds of thunderclaps put together, shook the house to its foundations. He stood there stunned, then with a speed that belied his years, flung open the window and shutters. Outside, the world was the same as always.

Paul said the island looked just like an aircraft carrier. Al laughed. That was what everyone said. A natural aircraft carrier created by God. (If God existed, why didn't he stop the war instead of making aircraft-carrier islands?) It was flat except for an elevated patch in the southeast corner, which dropped straight down three or four hundred feet into the Pacific. The Japs had been cornered there and many had jumped off the cliff to their death, Paul related. His small eyes sparkled amid his large face, just as Al remembered them. The island was like Manhattan, Al suggested. There was a Broadway with Thirty-fourth and Forty-second streets, and even Times Square. Paul grinned and nodded.

Al had been drinking a beer in the PX bar when a black man in Navy uniform walked in. Al looked at him suspiciously, wondering why a Navy man had come into the Army bar. The sailor's enormous face wore a big grin, but the first feature Al noticed were the eyes that shone like glass beads.

"Golden Eagle!" Al first exclaimed. He had meant to say the sailor's name, but instead the location to which the face belonged came out. He couldn't forget the bar he often took Susan to on their dates. Or Larry, the barman. It was where he had declared to Will that he was going off to the war. There was Ken, who had taken over the ranch. And the grouchy Mr. Griggs; Huey, the trapper; Susan's sister, Peggy; and of course Peggy's self-appointed lover Joe. . . . Images came flooding back like a word-association game.

Al had met Joe once on the aircraft-carrier island. "What? The Runner came here?" Paul exclaimed in a voice befitting his large face.

They looked at one another and laughed, one a big black face, the other, a white—no, tanned by now from the tropical sun—face, half the size of the other.

Paul asked the obvious question as he started on a beer himself. "What was he doing here?"

"Fighting a war," Al laughed. "We're winning, the Japs are retreating, slowly but surely, toward the northeast. We've pushed them back this far at least." He stressed the we, because he had taken part in the battle to land on the island. The Japanese had put up suicidal resistance. His friend fighting next to him had had his head blown off by machine-gun fire. Al was lucky: He had escaped with a slight wound in his shoulder. It was only because of the fierce fighting of ground soldiers like them that they now had the world's largest base on the aircraft-carrier island.

Paul listened in silence as one by one he emptied the cans of beer on the table. Choosing his moment, he asked, "How many of those big ones they got here?" He was obviously referring to the B-29 super-fortress bombers that had been leveling the Jap cities. Al said he was only guarding the base, but according to a friend of his from a B-29 crew, they had more than a thousand. "Wait a minute," Paul interjected. "You say you're guarding this place. Are you trying to tell me the Japs are going to come back again?"

"They're still out there, you know, and they're starving."

Now and then they came out under cover of darkness. They were not strong enough to attack the base, but they carried out their night raids on the base's food dump, frantically carrying away any scraps they could find. Sometimes Al's friends retaliated with their own night raids on Jap soldiers. Most were hiding in caves in the jungle. The Americans threw grenades into the caves and shot them as they ran out. Al didn't take part in the game, but some of his friends really enjoyed it. They dragged crew members of the big ones along with them too. Since the crew members were free except when they were off razing Jap cities, and had nothing to relieve their boredom except poker and fighting, they got a kick out of "Jap-hunting." Some boasted about how many they had shot the previous night. Al thought it was strange that they should brag about hunting three or four miserable Japs when they were out killing thousands—tens of thousands—at a time on their raids.

"Did Joe run here too?" Paul grinned impishly. "These runways would be ideal for it."

"Hmm, I wonder," chuckled Al. He certainly had no desire to run along the enormous concrete runways that cut through the jungle, but having been speed-crazy during his youth, he would have loved to race a car along them. He used to race with his friends in jalopies on the desert, but there they could never get up much speed. Here the solid runways stretching right to the cliffs would have been perfect. He would look at them gleaming at night on guard duty and picture his own car racing down the runway as fast as the big ones taking off.

It was after one of these fantasies that Al had met Joe. He was on his way back to his quarters from night duty. The birds had started up in the twilight before sunrise and a silhouette could be seen standing near his billet, with the noisy tropical jungle as a backdrop. He could not make out who it was at first, but the figure suddenly moved toward him.

"Al—it's me, Joe," the figure greeted him. It was a hurried reunion. Joe had arrived the previous evening from his mainland base via Hawaii and was leaving for Okinawa that morning. Quite by accident he had learned Al was on the island and had come looking for him. "They said you were on patrol, so I had to come back at dawn." The two embraced and slapped each other on the back. Joe then provided a quick account of what he had been up to. He had been to Europe and Africa.

"Hey, so you've been checking out the English girls, eh?" Al teased him.

"Come off it." Joe feigned a punch. "I was mostly in North Africa, in the desert." There had been women there but their mouths, noses, and even their eyes had been swathed in black cloth. Maybe that was just as well. Black clothes made them look mysterious, but sometimes they concealed leprosy. The Germans were defeated and the war in Europe was over. They had thought they might be able to go home at last, but ended up going right through America without stopping, except for one week's leave, which Joe spent back at their town. It wasn't exactly his hometown, but it seemed like home anyway.

He had visited the Golden Eagle and Susan's house as well—or should he say Peggy's? Peggy had been completely caught off guard by his sudden appearance. She sat riveted to her sister's side and could hardly open her mouth. Ken let him stay in his old room at the ranch. That was nice of him, but he still didn't like Ken. The old attic room he liked so much that looked right out over the ranch was now being used by a Mexican seasonal laborer. Mexicans must have no tradition of keeping, or desire to keep, their rooms clean. God knows what he had spilled on it; the floor was a dirty black and the wallpaper torn everywhere.

When the week was up and he was about to board the Greyhound bus to California from the station near Susan's house, Peggy came running to him, crying, "Why didn't you tell me you were leaving?" Tears welled up in her large, round eyes (Susan always teased her about those eyes, which bore a permanent look of surprise). Joe hated emotional farewells, so he had told no one of his exact departure date.

"How could you do this? I hope the Japs take you prisoner and cut your head off with a big sword!" she said choking as he mounted the steps of the bus.

"The Japs won't get me." He turned and waved at her freckled, tear-stained face.

Joe was normally a man of few words, especially compared to the voluble Al, but as they sat on the rock outside Al's billet that morning, it was Joe who did most of the talking.

Al got a word in: "Where are you going now?"

"Well, we stopped off here to refuel. Then we're off to Okinawa, and after that, we're going to drop bombs on Japan." The bomber he had flown over in as rear gunner was one size smaller than the big ones. If they were super aerial fortresses, his was just an aerial fortress. Its cruising range was shorter too. Japan was out of range from the aircraft-carrier island, but not from Okinawa. As he spoke, the birds started up in the jungle and a shower of morning cries rained down on them.

A funny question lodged itself in Al's mind. If all Joe was going to do was fly over Japan, could he actually say he had been to Japan? He remained silent; after all, Joe would laugh and call it typical landlubber thinking. But however many bombs they might drop, that alone was not going to decide the outcome of the war. It had been true for the aircraft-carrier island, just as it had been for Okinawa, where Joe was now headed. The infantry, with men like Al, still had to move in and fight to capture places like that.

"I feel as if I've been doing all this fighting just to send you off to Japan," he said instead.

It was like a relay, with so many lives lost along the way. Al and his lot were the runners, Joe and his were the baton. When one runner fell, he desperately tried to pass the baton on to the next. When that runner fell, he passed the baton on, and so on. Starting from Guadalcanal, the runners had passed through myriads of little islands as far as Okinawa, where the baton by the name of Joe was about to be passed to the last runner for the home stretch to the Jap mainland.

When Al told Paul that Joe had gone to Okinawa, Paul talked about his cruiser's role in the capture of the island. "I wasn't on it, myself," he said, and explained how the cruiser was hit by a kamikaze plane—only one, but it was enough to open up a big hole. Twenty people had died. It had had to undergo major repairs in Hawaii before returning to the mainland. Most of the crew were relieved, and Paul was in the new crew.

"It's an old boat, you know. They've done it up with radar and other stuff, but it's top-heavy. Some say one torpedo and that'll be it." The old top-heavy boat had come over at full speed, carrying secret weapons as cargo; they were long, cylindrical objects accompanied by two Army officers. Even the military police were guarding them.

"What sort of secret weapons?"

"Who knows? Some kind of rocket, I guess." The two accompanying officers in fact looked more like Army doctors, so some of Paul's friends thought they were for germ warfare.

"Whatever they are, I guess they'll kill plenty of Japs."

"Yeah." Paul nodded, forcing the opener into another can of beer.

"You drink a lot," laughed Al.

Paul nodded again. "Yeah."

"I don't know about secret weapons, but all kinds of things are needed for war, and all kinds of people," Al mused, with a hint of irony in his voice. There was one group which did not go off to Japan with the others but just went around bombing neighboring islands. They would load their big ones with a single bomb, drop it on starving Jap soldiers holed up in the jungle, and come back again. Al thought it was a waste of time, but they always got special treatment. Their captain was only twenty-nine, but he was a cut above all the other captains, wielding authority above and beyond the other squadron leaders. They had finally started going to Japan, but not in convoy with the others, to raze the Jap cities: They went off one by one, dropped their single bomb, and scurried back as fast as they could. One of them came back recently bragging that he had bombed Hirohito's palace in Tokyo. With Hirohito dead, the war would be over, he declared. He must have scuttled some poor Jap wood-and-paper houses and obliterated a few families instead.

Al began singing:

*Into the air the secret rose,*
*Where they're going, nobody knows.*
*Tomorrow they'll return again,*
*But we'll never know where they've been.*
*Don't ask us about results or such,*
*Unless you want to get in Dutch.*

Paul frowned, then burst out laughing in the middle. "What the heck's that?"

"Everyone knows it here. It's called 'Nobody Knows.' I don't know who wrote it but the words are pretty good." Al hummed it again, to Paul's continued amusement.

Paul shook his head. "War's a strange thing. If it weren't for the war, neither of us would be here in the middle of the tropics."

"You're not kidding. And Joe wouldn't be going to Okinawa. And only the big shots and the rich would get to go and see Fujiyama and the geishas." From his expression, Paul had not heard about Fujiyama or geishas. "We'd have nothing to do with Hirohito's country," rephrased Al.

Paul nodded. "That's what Daniel said." Before joining his top-heavy cruiser and coming all the way to this island, which he would never have come to otherwise, he had gone home for a few days' leave. A friend had taken him along to church, where he met Daniel, who said he would probably be going to war soon, too, as an Army chaplain. Daniel had asked God to protect Paul while he fought, then joked that, thanks to the war, they could travel to places they would normally never be able to see. One of his seminary friends had ended up on a tiny island; war wasn't completely bad.

"Who knows? Maybe he's here too," Al interrupted. The talk of Daniel had reminded him of Susan. They had made their vows before Daniel, but they were already broken. She had sent him a letter saying that their personalities did not match, and that it would be better for both of them if they separated. Of course it was just an excuse. Joe had said to him when they met, "You should give up that Susan." He might have wanted to say that she was playing around with other men. And if Paul had just come back, why didn't he say something about her? He must have also heard some bad rumors. Al changed the subject. "I wonder how many times Joe's been to Japan."

"Hmm, I wonder." Paul picked up his beer again. "The Japs don't have many fighters now, do they? They don't have many anti-aircraft guns, either, and what they do have don't hit. . . . It's a one-sided war. We're beating the shit out of them and they're doing nothin'," he said, emptying the can.

Al hesitated a second before agreeing. A strange image had formed in his mind—the same relay image as before, with each runner falling and trying desperately to pass the baton on to the next runner, only this time they must have come to the last of the runners, because the baton suddenly started running on its own. The baton had become the Runner. And the Runner was Joe—running for all he was worth toward Japan, the unknown land of the people who lived in houses made of paper and wood, which, but for the war, he would never be going to. The Runner was bounding across the sea, as if he were racing across the desert expanse of White Sands. Run, Joe—Joe, the Runner!

It was almost two years since George had gone to prison. It was two and a half years since he and five youths from his tribe had refused their draft orders and were arrested by the police. George could still remember it vividly. He had returned as usual with his sheep from the plain below one evening to find the local police waiting for him. They handcuffed him and took him into town. On the way he was offered some Coca-Cola and crackers for dinner, which he ate while still handcuffed. An Army officer, a veritable mountain twice their size, was waiting for him and the others with draft forms. Sign and you won't have to go to prison, he had told them, threatened them—even implored them—but all six had shaken their heads. If they signed those forms there would be no rebirth for them into the next world. They were not refusing for themselves but for the whole of their tribe, they told him.

"We are not taking this action because someone encouraged us. Our elders didn't encourage us. We're acting on our convictions," George began, in his statement in court. They had to act in accordance with their religious principles. When their ancestors came into this Fourth World after the destruction of the Third, they promised their Protector never to take up weapons for destruction. If we take up arms, we will never be born into the Fifth World after the destruction of the unruly Fourth, he had declared to the court.

The all-white jury—none of the faces were black or yellow—appeared singularly unimpressed. George had thought about Chuck, who had taught him the legends of his tribe. He had died within three months of being returned to the reservation. Once his Gale clan had finished gathering wood, building homes, and settling in at the top of the mountain, he hardly ever spoke. He seemed overcome by a sense of futility. Then one day he just got up and started running, dragging his old legs along the steep path connecting the mountain range to the desert.

"Where are you going? Training for the Olympics again? This is no time for Olympics—we're in a war," people said to him, but he carried on as if possessed. He ran down to the desert, then up the mountain again. He ran all day long, and finally even at night. One night he never came back. Early the next morning they started combing the ranges and the desert in search of him. It was Ron who found the old man's body at the foot of a precipice that afternoon. It looked as though he had strayed off the track and fallen over, except the moon had been full and exceptionally bright the night before, so he should have been able to see his way. Some said he had committed suicide, but Ron was adamant that his uncle would never take his own life. He must have fallen over the precipice and died.

Ron did not say, though, that he had tripped accidentally. "Uncle believed that this world had come to its end," he declared. He had been looking for the hole of the Ant People, where his clan could take shelter until the birth of the new world. "Didn't you hear what Uncle Chuck said?" he rebuked his incredulous older brother. "Or don't you believe what he said about the beginning of the new world?"

It wasn't that George disbelieved his uncle. Rather, he had completely forgotten his uncle's tale about the Creation. Before his brother's reproachful glower, he had felt a sense of shame and anger such as he had never experienced before. It was this feeling that later prompted his decision to follow the ancient teachings of his tribe never to take up arms.

Chuck must have seen the Ant People, Ron had insisted. When he came to the precipice he heard the Mochni bird's haunting cry. Then he heard the voice of Sótuknang alerting him that the end of this strife-ridden world was near. Ron spoke as if he were merely stating the obvious. Chuck and his clan were to prepare to live in the new world inside the anthill. Sótuknang had instructed him to look out from the bottom of the precipice toward the desert in the south-east, which stretched as far as White Sands. His *kópavi* had become soft, so he could hear the voice of Sótuknang and see into the distance. He could make out the soft mound of the anthill in the middle of the desert, and the Ant People beside it, beckoning to him. "You and your clan will be saved because, like your ancestors before you, you have observed the teaching never to take up arms against one another," Sótuknang told him.

"You mean Uncle Chuck just stepped out into space?" George protested. At that time he still had not decided for certain to refuse the draft. Ron nodded. "That's right." To their uncle it looked as if the ground stretched all the way from his feet to the anthill. It was only natural that he would step out over the precipice.

"Do you really think this is the end of the world?"

"The end, brother," Ron replied with conviction. "Doesn't the world look as red as the sun—or a fireball hundreds of times brighter? The people are being burned alive, becoming charred corpses." There was fear now in Ron's eyes, as if he actually saw the ball of fire. "After the fire comes water. A black rain will fall on the waste, and mud will flow over the earth."

"So what are you going to do?"

"I'm waiting for Sótuknang. When my *kópavi* tells me, I'll go to the anthill."

"And what if your *kópavi* doesn't tell you?" George glanced at his little brother, who somehow didn't seem so little anymore.

"It will," Ron replied, as though it were as certain as his growing facial hair. He touched his upper lip, already bearing faint traces of a mustache, and stroked it affectionately.

All this flashed through George's mind as he spoke in the courtroom. Even if the all-white jury became convinced that the measly Indians in front of them had taken leave of their senses, he had to tell them of their irrevocable decision.

His parents had been upset that he would be jailed, but then agreed he should follow his beliefs. He had told the jury how difficult it would be for him to leave his elderly parents to go off to prison. Who could tell how many years they and his little brother would have to look after the animals by themselves? (He could see Ron's steely eyes again. George had not told him about his decision. No doubt his brother took it for granted.) Nevertheless, by not taking up arms and by killing no one, they would secure a place in the new world. Such was their belief. This time George had spoken as if he were stating the obvious and felt inwardly pleased. He ended on an ironic note:

"The law says that if you kill someone you go to jail. It seems we're being sent to prison because we *won't* kill anyone."

There was provision in the law for conscientious objectors. Had they been white like the jury and refused the draft for religious reasons like the Quakers, maybe they would not have gone to prison. But the jury was not going to see their tribal teachings in the same light. It was a foregone conclusion that George and his friends would be imprisoned.

Life behind closed walls is hard for anyone, but it was unbearably difficult for the Indian youths accustomed to tending their animals outdoors. On occasions when they were taken outside to work, they were marched through the town in handcuffs, displayed to passersby as common criminals. It was not easy to find consolation in the belief that they were there to be reborn into the new world.

Among the whites, Mexicans, and Negroes in the prison, they were the only Indians. Although they were not mistreated, they were often laughed at. After lights-out at nine o'clock, George would gather the other five in a corner of their communal room to reassure them that they were not alone, that their Protector was there with them. He tried to encourage himself as much as them. When they had fallen asleep, he would pray and ask the Protector to send a sign, to show he really was with them.

For a long time George's earnest prayers went unheeded. Doubts began to creep into his mind, in spite of his continued praying every night. It was at the beginning of their second long summer in jail that the sign came. They saw it through the little window of the communal room—a ball of fire flying slowly from the north and disappearing into the south. For four nights in a row the ball appeared. They knew it was the sign they had been waiting for by the mysterious energy each of them felt. The next day when they were out repairing roads with the other inmates, a drill got stuck in a hard rock and no one could get it out, not even the muscular Negroes in their group. As they formed a circle around the drill, someone joked, "Why don't the Indians have a go?" and everyone burst out laughing. They stopped when George stepped forward and took hold of it.

"All right, let me try," he said. He closed his eyes for a second and prayed, not for himself but so that the others could see that the Indians were humans too. He braced himself, pulled, and the bit came free.

Early in the morning, four days later, something roused George and told him to look out the window. He stood on tiptoe and peered outside. At that very instant the sky to the south lit up as brightly as the midday sun. The light faded, but the image stayed in his eyes. He closed them, trying to work out what it meant. As he did so, an earsplitting sound, like hundreds of thunderclaps all at once, broke the silence. It could not be a sign. Or, if it was, then the world was ending and a new one about to begin. But he still had not heard the voice of Sótuknang. Maybe it was a munitions depot exploding somewhere. George felt fear in his heart.

A few days later he was told that his sister had come to visit. Surprised, he made for the interview room and found a depressed-looking Laura sitting in the corner. It was by no means easy for her to come this far, but George knew immediately that it was not the trip that was weighing on her.

"What's the matter?"

"It's Ron. . . .

"What happened? Is he dead?" George was surprised at his own impulsiveness. Laura shook her head listlessly.

"He's gone mad." He had also gone blind, and all he would say was "I saw it! I saw it!" When they asked him what he saw, he said the end of the world. Then he babbled on about people dancing—men dancing as though they were crazy. No, before that she had to say that he had been missing for several days. He suddenly left the house and did not return. Thinking he must have collapsed on the desert, the whole clan went out to look for him, but in vain. When news reached Laura that their elderly parents were sick from worry, she dropped everything and hurried back to the reservation, praying desperately in the bus that Ron would be all right. As though her prayers had been answered, the night she arrived, Ron was brought back by the police. A patrolman had spotted him wandering along the road near White Sands two mornings before, as if he were sleepwalking.

"He says he saw a ball of fire and the world has come to an end." The policeman sighed as he looked at Ron. He was sympathetic for a white.

"If the world has come to an end, does that mean a new one is beginning?"

Ron, who had been staring into space (it was then that Laura and her parents realized he was unable to see), broke his silence. "The Fifth World has already started," he cried. Ron claimed he had been blinded by a flaming fireball, the result of a trick by Huey, the trapper. On the day he disappeared, he was walking along the track near the spot where Chuck had fallen over the precipice. He thought he heard Chuck's voice, but it could have been Sótuknang, for the sound came from his *kópavi*. The voice told him to go immediately to the altar Chuck, George, and he had built in the desert.

He ran down the mountain and across the desert as far as the highway. A truck carrying ore from the mine near the reservation gave him a lift to the main road, where he hitched another ride, and so on to White Sands, or at least to the chain-link fence around the vast training area. He had asked to be let off there. The friendly truck driver put on the brakes. "What are you going to do around here? Play with the coyotes?" he asked. "That's right. I'm going to play with the coyotes," Ron chirped back, then added under his breath, "before the end of the world comes."

"Good luck," the driver said, slapping him on the back. "You'd better be careful if you're going in there. There've been lots of vehicles going in and out. The other day I saw a big container brought in on a trailer. I don't know what's going on, but"— he gestured with his chin to the white expanse of desert on the other side of the fence—"the Army is up to something."

Ron scaled the wire fence with ease and set off to find the underground altar. The truck driver was right: A lot of vehicles were coming and going. They were stopped by soldiers and looked as if they were being inspected as they came in. Ron knew the desert like the back of his hand, so he could evade the guards. In the distance he could see a strange metal scaffold and next to it the large receptacle-like metal object the driver had told him about. A crowd was gathered around it, some in Army uniforms, but most looking like civilians.

The altar was some distance from the tower. Chuck had told Ron just before his death that Huey had discovered it. Ron was worried that Huey had told the authorities, and half expected to find it destroyed. He needn't have feared. It was just as they had left it. He let out a whoop of delight and jumped inside to offer a prayer of thanksgiving.

For how many hours or days Ron stayed there, no one knew. Outside the hole nothing happened or even looked about to happen. He began to feel uncertain. Was it really Chuck's voice or Sótuknang he had heard? Or was it an illusion? If it was Sótuknang, where were the Ant People? As he gave it more thought, certain inconsistencies dawned on him. If this was the anthill, why had his *kópavi* not told him to bring his parents? If he were going to be reborn into the Fifth World, what about George, who was in jail for following their ancestors' teachings? What about Laura, who was so worried about George? Shouldn't they all be there too?

As he slumped into a fit of despair at the bottom of the hole, he heard a voice from above. He could not make out the first faint sounds, but as it grew louder he realized it was a countdown: "Ten . . . nine . . ."

At the same moment, another voice, a familiar one, shouted, "Come out, Ron." Ron knew in an instant that the voice belonged to Huey. "I'm not listening to you," he shouted back, but Huey's next words brought him climbing the half-broken ladder to the surface. "Are you afraid of the Japs too? Your brother was so afraid of them he went to jail. Are you chicken like him? The Japs have come to rape your sister, Laura!"

Of course the Japs had not arrived. The very instant Ron realized Huey had tricked him, there was a tremendous flash of light. It sent him tumbling back to the bottom of the ladder. He was fortunate, for a few seconds later a wind powerful enough to carry anything before it swept across the desert with a deafening roar. If he had been aboveground he might have been blown to pieces. He regained his senses and scrambled up the ladder once more. His vision was already dimmed from the brilliant light, but like a blurred film, his eyes made out some men in the distance dancing madly as if performing a primitive rite. People must dance like that either at the beginning of the world or the end, he thought. No sound accompanied the spectacle. After the great boom the desert was enveloped in a primordial silence, and the dancers looked like figures in a shadow play. Then darkness closed in on Ron's vision.

"I wonder what did happen?" George asked slowly, looking intently at his sister after she had finished recounting her story.

"I don't know," Laura replied, returning his gaze.

"This world isn't finished. . . ."

Laura was silent for a moment. "The new one hasn't begun." That was for certain, she continued. Ron was very sick. Two or three days after coming home he had broken out in a fever. His hair had began to fall out, and in a couple of days he had become completely bald, like an old man.

"What the heck was going on there?" George asked again slowly.

"I don't know," Laura said again. Fear showed in her eyes, the same as must surely be in his, he thought.

The green contours of the land below—Jap country—had seemed very remote from the vantage point of the plane up until now. But suddenly they were all-important. As the green drew slowly but inexorably closer, fear superimposed an image on it, one from a photograph Joe had seen of a Jap soldier with a huge sword decapitating a Chinese prisoner. He had heard that such a fate awaited all those seized by the Japs.

"We'll just have to make sure we're not captured, that's all. God knows how we can do that!" Captain Lewis laughed. That had been just before they left Kadena Air Base on Okinawa that night. Of course he was sure it would never happen to him or his crew of nine. They all laughed, including Joe, though he had felt uneasy.

The Jap defenses were by now so weak that fighters presented no threat, and there was little danger from anti-aircraft guns. This was their third mission over Japan, and most of them felt they knew all they needed to know about the enemy. Before the first mission, even the easygoing Captain Lewis had been tense. He had ordered a cleaning-out of the plane—it would be embarrassing if they were shot down with empty condom packets in the corner of the cockpit. They didn't find any condoms in the cleanup, but a pair of black and pink panties did turn up. No one knew where they had come from. Maybe they belonged to someone's girlfriend, or maybe someone had crept into the women's quarters and stolen them. Joe brandished them in front of Captain Lewis's nose:

"Black and pink—they would make good semaphore flags. Let's keep them." Captain Lewis, usually open to bantering with his crew, curtly told him to throw them away.

On the third bombing mission the craft had not been cleaned; there might very well be some funny things on board. Such thoughts were no longer occupying Joe's mind, for at this moment the two engines on the right were spewing out flames, half the tail was gone and they were losing altitude fast. He searched the terrain below, looking for some means of refuge.

Before that day he had never heard of the naval port of Kure, much less most of the cities they were ordered to bomb. (The captain and the navigator had to search for them on maps, but to rear gunner Joe, shut up in the back of the plane on the lookout for interceptors, the names meant nothing.) There were still a few surviving battleships stationed there apparently, and they had come all the way to bomb the biggest of these. And a long way it was—far enough from Okinawa, far far away from the United States, and a world away from White Sands. He had come all this way to get hit by antiaircraft fire and to plummet toward Jap soil below.

This isn't part of the deal, a voice inside him shouted. What the deal was or who it was with was not clear, but this was not part of it. Al—he had made a deal with him when they met on the aircraft-carrier island. Actually, it was more a wager: to see who would be first to reach Jap country. The clamor of the tropical birds early that morning by Al's billet came back to him. Why had they made the wager? Joe had said naturally he would be first to reach Japan. After all, they weren't going to Okinawa for fun. They were going to bomb the Jap mainland.

"You can't call that going to Japan. Going to Japan means putting both feet on Japanese soil." Al had stamped his feet to emphasize the point. "You should run on Japanese soil like you did back home," he teased Joe. It was then that they made the bet. "I tell you what: If you get there first, when you get a ranch somewhere, I'll pay one-fifth—no, make that one-tenth of it."

"Okay. If you get there first, I'll buy your wife—" Remembering all the rumors going round about Susan when he went back, Joe corrected himself. "No, I'll buy *you* . . . drinks for six months at the Golden Eagle."

Just five days before, on Okinawa, Joe had received a letter from Al, telling him of his meeting with Paul. Now rumor had it that Paul's cruiser had been torpedoed by the Japanese on its way home to the mainland. Al didn't know the details. The rest of the letter was scrawled, unlike Al's usual careful handwriting, hinting that he was in a confused state of mind. "All we can do now is pray for that nigger's safety. His boat brought some weird weapon to our island—they say it can end the war with one blast. I doubt it myself. We've still got to do our fighting before we get to go home. Like I told you about the relay, it looks like Paul's down—I hope he's not—but I'm still okay, and we've got to get you to Japan. The words *Good luck* were scrawled at the bottom. Joe could see those words superimposed on the green world below. Suddenly the strained voice of Captain Lewis sounded in his headset.

"Come up here. We're going to bail out."

"Yes, sir," Joe responded in a subdued tone. He threw on his parachute and clambered through the narrow passageway connecting the tail with the front of the craft, where the other eight crew members were already assembled.

"Prepare to jump," the captain ordered.

Dick, the navigator, was the first to go; Joe was third. His training had taught him to kick out powerfully against the oncoming wind. As he braced himself he heard one of the crew ask, "Where are we?" and Captain Lewis's reply: "The outskirts of Hiroshima." The outskirts of Hiroshima—those words rang in his ears as he looked to the world below. He was not going to let the Japs catch him. When he hit ground he was going to run as hard as he could. Dear God, help me run, he prayed.

509th Composite Group
Office of the Operation
Officer APO 247
c/o Postmaster, San Francisco, California
5 August 1945

**Operation order Number 35**
**Date of Mission: 6 August 1945**

| | | |
|---|---|---|
| Briefings: | See below | |
| Takeoff | Weather Ships | at 0200 (approx) |
| | Strike Ships | at 0300 (approx) |
| Out of Sacks | Weather | at 2230 |
| | Strike | at 2330 |
| Mess | | 2315 to 0115 |
| Lunches | 39 | at 2320 |
| | 52 | at 0030 |
| Trucks | 3 | at 0015 |
| | 4 | at 0115 |

| A/C No. | Victor No. | Apco |
|---|---|---|
| Weather Mission | | |
| 298 | 83 | Taylor |
| 303 | 71 | Wilson |
| 301 | 85 | Eatherly |
| 302 | 72 | Alternate A. C. |
| | | |
| Combat Strikes | | |
| 292 | 82 | Tibbets |
| 353 | 89 | Sweeney |
| 291 | 91 | Marquardt |
| 354 | 90 | McKnight |
| 304 | 88 | Alternate for Marquardt |

| | | |
|---|---|---|
| Gas | 82 | 7000 gals |
| | All others | 7400 gals |
| Bombs | Special | |
| Religious Service | Catholic | at 2200 |
| | Protestant | at 2230 |

"Almighty Father, Who wilt hear the prayer of them that love Thee, we pray Thee to be with those who brave the heights of Thy heaven and who carry the battle to our enemies. Guard and protect them, we pray Thee, as they fly their appointed rounds. May they, as well as we, know Thy strength and power, and armed with Thy might may they bring this war to a rapid end. We pray Thee that the end of the war may come soon, and that once more we may know peace on earth. May the men who fly this night be kept safe in Thy care, and may they be returned safely to us. We shall go forward trusting in Thee, knowing that we are in Thy care now and forever. In the Name of Jesus Christ. Amen."

Iwata Kyoko set out early that morning to visit Abdullah Hassan in the suburban hospital. She was visiting the Indonesian student at the request of her secret lover of the past two years, Shindo Isamu.

Shindo had been a student, too, when they first met, but was now a soldier in the local Hiroshima Regiment. Things were better now that he had become a private first class, but in the beginning when she met him on rare leaves, his cheeks would be badly swollen.

"Whatever has happened to you?" she once asked naively.

"Slaps on the face—it's part of the great tradition of the

Japan Imperial Army." Shindo grimaced, trying to laugh. "We've been doing a lot of losing lately. The enemy's too strong, so they start picking on the weaker ones on their own side."

"What's going to happen?"

"The war will be over soon." His candid remark shocked her, and his next words even more: "Japan will be beaten."

She stiffened and glared at her lover, but in truth the idea had been mulling inside her for some time now. "Are we really going to lose?"

"We're already suffering defeat after defeat, aren't we?"

"What will become of us?"

"Nothing much." He stared fixedly into space, and she tried to follow his gaze. "Kyo-chan, just look at history. There's always been fighting somewhere. Some countries win and some lose; it's natural, isn't it? Even if a country loses, the people live on. What's that they say—'A country is defeated but the rivers and mountains remain'? You just keep on living."

"But Isamu-san . . ." It was the first time she had used his first name. She had always called him Shindo-san, even when he embraced her. "What about you? Are you going to . . . ?" She was hoping for a pledge from him.

"I'll live," he said.

Upon being promoted to private first class, Shindo got leave once a month. As soon as he left the camp he would head straight for Iwata Kyoko's tiny four-and-a-half—tatami-mat room in a tiny wooden apartment building. They would come together and devour each other's body greedily. The cries and groans of their lovemaking must have been audible through the flimsy wooden walls, but they did not care.

"The military police will come if we're not careful," he laughed. The thought had also crossed her mind. If they came she would demand to know if there was a law forbidding lovers to embrace. The thought made her seek him all the more passionately.

She first met him on the *T*-shaped bridge one lunchtime. She had strolled there from her office and was looking down into the lazy current of water.

"Peaceful, isn't it? You'd hardly know there's a war on," a voice next to her said. She looked up to see a young man in a sweater, unusual for that time of year. Men often talked to her on the street (she must have looked like that type of girl), but not to Kikuko, who was much prettier. She would customarily tell them off, but something in the way the young man spoke stopped her this time. Their conversation was short, but it was enough to find out each other's names. He learned that she had graduated from a girls' high school and then been mobilized to the Supplies Control Association as a female volunteer. She learned that he was a university student.

"I may be a student, but I've been mobilized like you. I'm a laborer now." The word *laborer* sounded novel. People had stopped using it, preferring *work soldier* or *worker*. "Lucky I skipped work today, otherwise I wouldn't have met you." Both laughed. When she asked if he was a native of Hiroshima, as she was, he replied that he was from an island to the south.

"So you're a fisherman's son."

"No, I'm sorry to say." His strong, protruding jaw melted into a grin. "I'm a shopkeeper's son."

He suggested casually that they meet at ten o'clock on their next day off. Equally casually, she agreed to the early-morning meeting. Both knew it would mean spending the whole day together. They would meet on the bridge.

"But what if there's an air raid? This bridge would make a good target, you know," she said, laughing.

He joined in her laughter. "I'll be here come hell or high water."

Iwata Kyoko was known for her high spirits and was thought to have several boyfriends. Actually there was no one she felt particularly close to, and contrary to the imaginations of the men at the office, she was still a virgin. Despite her risqué jokes with them, she had yet to experience even her first kiss.

Whenever a man came close, she felt uneasy, almost as though she had some kind of male phobia. Perhaps that was why she became domineering in their presence. But with Shindo she could be relaxed and open. Even so, although they continued to meet on their days off, it was a long time before they exchanged their first kiss. He had come to her apartment and sampled her cooking (which admittedly was nothing special, and he told her so), but they had done no more than hold hands.

They became intimate when he was drafted into the Army. But they had few chances to meet. She sometimes wondered how many other young couples like them there must be in Japan. Perhaps quite a number, but since Japan was a society where even a young man and woman walking together in the street was frowned upon, there was no way of telling. She felt as though they had been cut off from Japanese society and that Japan had become their enemy.

Neither of them talked about marriage. She was not sure how he felt, and under such tense wartime conditions she could not bring the subject up. He talked of being sent south soon. To mention marriage, a product of peace, would defile the love that existed between them. She couldn't begin to understand Kikuko, having a marriage meeting just as in peacetime, then having a wedding a few months later at the famous Itsukushima Shrine, albeit scaled down a bit. On top of that, she had married an active lieutenant, a man who was supposed to be out fighting at the front (or maybe should have been dead already, Kyoko sometimes thought irritably). When Kyoko visited her the other day she was already behaving like a domesticated housewife, not one month after marriage. She seemed completely at home amid their little second-floor nest for newlyweds.

"Isn't your husband going south?" Kyoko asked, not meaning to be sarcastic.

"I've no idea. I don't know about such things," Kikuko replied. Her self-composure suggested that even if her husband were to be sent south to the front, she would send him off with a dutiful smile. Kyoko wondered how she would react in a similar situation. She recalled a scene from the movie *Morocco,* which she had pestered her cousin to take her to before the war broke out. A woman chased her legionnaire lover across the desert and eventually collapsed in the sand. She didn't know whether she would go that far. No, of course, she wouldn't . . . and if she did, it would be useless anyway. Still, there was something in her that might push her to try. It must be love. The thought occupied her mind while she answered Kikuko's questions about her friends at the office.

When Shindo came to see her about a week later, she asked him about Kikuko's husband. He shook his head and laughed. "Kyo-chan, you don't know anything, do you? In the Army, a first lieutenant is a god. We're supposed to grovel in front of them. When I was out in the sticks—you know what I mean by the sticks: the world outside the Army, like here . . ." He patted the mat between them as they sat facing each other. "They think the Army is at the center of the world and everything else is the sticks. When I was out in the sticks I thought first lieutenants were just ordinary soldiers. But when I joined the Army, they became gods."

"So you didn't take the officer's exam because you weren't interested in becoming a god?" she teased him.

"You may be right." He smiled wryly. The word god reminded him of Homer's epic.

"You know the Iliad, don't you, Kyo-chan?" She vaguely remembered mention of it in her high school history book and nodded. Shindo had studied western history at the university, so he was well versed in such topics, but he didn't often talk about them. This was one of his rare moments of nostalgia. In the beginning there was a passage about the gods who, in their anger at the arrogance of man, showered arrows down upon them. These arrows of anger turned into arrows of fire, which destroyed the towns below. The people had no defense against the arrows of the gods, and ran about in panic and confusion, searching for an escape.

"I can't help thinking that's what's happening to Japan right now," he said in a low voice.

Kyoko was uncertain how to respond, but Shindo changed the subject. Once the war was over, he hoped to travel to some of the islands in the Aegean Sea that provided the setting for those Greek epics. Maybe his attachment to the idea stemmed from the fact that he had been born and raised on an island in an inland sea too.

She beamed. "I'll go with you, Isamu-san."

His eyes suddenly lit up too. "Kyo-chan, do you realize the war over there's finished? That's right, the war's over. It's peacetime again!"

That conversation had taken place three days before. More than his words, she felt from his tone of voice that he was trying to convince himself it would soon be all over. All they needed was a little more patience. But the war was going to end with the defeat of Japan. What would happen then? What would become of the Japanese people, themselves included?

It was just past 7:00 a.m. as she walked along the road to the suburban hospital. Other than the occasional lot where an evacuated house had been pulled down, little appeared different from peacetime. But Kyoko felt utterly miserable. It was not the prospect of Japan's defeat that depressed her. Her body was now showing undeniable signs of pregnancy. She had tried to tell Shindo, but with all the talk of Kikuko's husband, flaming arrows raining down from the gods, and then the Aegean Sea, she could not find the right moment to tell him he was to be a father, fearing his reaction. He had stopped after saying his usual "Well, I've got to be off" and looked at her. "What's up?" he had asked.

She swallowed the words on the tip of her tongue and shook her head. "Nothing." Then she had said goodbye with her usual "Take care."

It was after talking about the Aegean Sea that Shindo had asked her to go and visit Abdullah Hassan. He and his friends at the university had organized a friendship group for exchange students from Southeast Asia. Kyoko was reminded of the dark youth who had passed her and Kikuko on the bridge and wondered if it might be the same person.

"It can be pretty rough when you're taken sick so far from home. Could you visit him for me? I don't know which hospital he's in, but you can find out if you go to his dormitory," Shindo said.

Mentioning foreigners having a rough time reminded him of the blindfolded prisoners he had seen a few days back, and he lowered his voice to tell her about it. They had been made to sit out on the parade ground. Several military police had grasped their hands at the back and jerked them up and down in a form of exercise. "Some planes were shot down over Kure the other day. The crews who parachuted were taken prisoner. Poor things. I suppose their heads will be cut off soon."

Kyoko had visited Hassan's dormitory the previous night after work and was told by another student where to find him. The student spoke excellent Japanese.

"Where do you come from?" she asked.

"Malaya," he smiled.

"What's wrong with Hassan-san? I hear it was sudden."

The student scratched his head. "He ate too much." The Asian students had started going to surrounding farms as volunteer laborers. For them it was too good an opportunity to miss. They were starving, like the Japanese. The farmers Hassan was helping were very generous. They invited him to eat as many pears as he wanted. He did just that, and became very sick. "That's what comes of making a pig of yourself." His fluency surprised her. "But he's Okay now. You can go and visit him."

Kyoko took some flowers to the hospital. It was impossible to obtain such luxuries in the city, but there were lots of flowers near Kikuko's home by the sea. Kikuko had arranged for her cousin Keiji to bring some in. Fortunately, Keiji had no classes that day, and was helping to demolish some evacuated buildings on the island by the T-shaped bridge. They met at the bridge and he handed her, considering the wartime conditions, an extravagant bouquet of flowers. They had obviously been carefully prepared by Kikuko's mother.

Keiji seemed much more cheerful than she had expected, in spite of his recent loss of both parents. He stood there with the bunch of flowers, looking decidedly bashful. From his expression she could imagine his embarrassment in the train on the way. They had met two or three times before, when he was with Kikuko, and exchanged a few words. This time he handed her the bouquet with an abrupt "Here you are" and, motioning to the row of buildings on the island, added impatiently, "I've got to get back to work."

Kyoko soon won over the nurse, who had insisted that visiting hours had not yet begun, and went to Hassan's bedside. He was sitting up, reading a book. Raising his head, he looked at her inquiringly. His face was much darker than that of his Malay friend and she felt mildly disappointed—he was definitely not the exchange student she had seen on the T-shaped bridge. She had just mentioned Shindo's name and was presenting him with the flowers when the young nurse hovering nearby gasped.

"What's that?" shouted a patient.

The young nurse, Kyoko, Hassan, and all the other patients in the room looked toward the open window as the air raid siren reverberated through the ward. In the cloudless summer sky they could make out a solitary glistening speck, unmistakably an enemy B-29 bomber, and then a black object falling from it. In the next instant the sky was lit up by a blinding burst of light. Instinctively, Kyoko threw herself to the floor. There followed an unearthly roar, as though the heavens were collapsing. The whole building shook and the windowpanes shattered. In that instant she did not think of Shindo. She thought of the seed planted in her womb. If I die, the baby will die too. I mustn't die. She did not pray, because the gods were already raining arrows of fire on them. Her only thought was: I will not die. I must live.

# II

* * *

He had no idea how or where he was walking; he only knew that the flames were pursuing him. How many days was it since he had been brought to this city? In solitary confinement the only thing he could see even in the daytime was the murky, dirty walls of the cell, illuminated by a dim electric bulb.

Once a day he had been taken outside for morning exercises, but then he was tightly blindfolded. Outside, though, he could at least hear things. First, he could hear them shouting commands. He could hear the sound of heavy boots marching, and the metallic sound of rifles striking against each other. He must have been in a barracks square or a drill ground. There he was made to sit while a guard stood behind him, moving his arms in a peculiar exercise routine.

Sometimes the sounds of the city had reached his ears, like the sound of distant waves. He tried to conjure up a picture of it while his arms were being moved about, but he could only imagine the cities of his own country. The cities here—Jap cities—were different. They had to be, even if there were people living in them.

Once, by divine mischief, the wind carried to him the distinct sounds of young women laughing. He tried to visualize them, but all he saw were girls from home. In the midst of them he saw precocious Peggy's freckled face, wearing the angry expression that had seen him off at the bus station. "I hope the Japs take you prisoner and cut your head off with a sword." Tears had streamed down her puffed-up cheeks.

"The Japs won't get me. Anyway, what's it got to do with you?" he had shot back. He often used to say that. While the guard was moving his arms up and down, he took himself back to when he was her age. "It's none of your business," he said, hands in his back pockets, thrusting his shoulders forward and spitting on the ground. "I'm getting out of here." He said it more to himself than to the girl. The war's nearly over, he thought. I'm going to meet those Jap girls. He opened his eyes wide under the blindfold, longing for a glimpse of them.

As if to prove his point, the siren started wailing. The guard, who could speak a little English, flung his arms down brusquely.

"Your planes coming to bomb us," he hissed. "They're coming to blow up your cities," Joe was on the point of saying, but checked himself. If he said it quickly enough the guard would not understand, but last time the siren went and he started to say something, someone had given him a savage blow on the side of his face.

"Your planes . . ." the guard repeated. Joe expected the usual "coming to bomb us," but this time it was ". . . coming to kill you." "Your country's planes coming to kill you," he said again and began laughing convulsively.

Three days had passed. It was a hot morning when the same English-speaking guard came to get him.

"Hot," said one.

"Hot," agreed the other. After this brief exchange, the guard led him along the usual path. Just as they began to step outside, the siren started wailing.

"Your planes . . ." the guard started. But before he could finish, a searing light pierced the blindfold, then everything went black.

* * *

He was squirming frantically under a heavy weight when he regained his senses. Struggling in the darkness, he eventually wriggled out from under what seemed to be a steel girder. He staggered out into the dazzling light. I can see! was his first thought. The blindfold had come off and he opened his eyes wide to look around.

But the world before him was torn apart, engulfed in flames. Beneath the flames the dark and silent earth lay exposed. Endless mounds of rubble were scattered over it. Here and there were black piles—scorched corpses. Some were white bones. As he struggled to take it all in, the flames roared up in a whirlwind, sweeping up the rubble, iron, glass and brick, the black piles and the white bones, into the black sky, then pelting them down mercilessly all around him. "Son!" he heard a voice call out. "Walk!" it commanded. It was somehow like Will's voice, but somehow not. "Walk, son." He began to stagger forward.

He was in the desert. It was White Sands, but the earth was black, devoid of the dry, stumpy grass. On the concrete crust of the earth, between the rubble and the flames, were piles of blackened corpses. He stumbled over them, not knowing where he was headed nor how to get his legs to carry him forward; all he knew was that he had to escape the flames pursuing him.

His vision blurred. Something was dripping profusely into his eyes. Maybe it was blood. He rubbed them with his hand, but each time something black stuck to it. Was it blood or mud? The flames were still raging, and the earth was as black as ever, but he saw it like an old, worn-out movie.

What was the time? The sky offered no clue. If I can find out the time I can survive, he thought, and began searching for some hint of the time of day. He found it—a scorched watch beside a black pile. He struggled to figure out the positions of the long hand and the short hand. Eight fifteen. The hands had stopped. Time had stopped there. As he began walking again a searing pain and heat spread through his body, and he was seized by a terrible thirst.

"Water," he croaked. "Give me water. *Mizu o kudasai.*" He had learned the Japanese in solitary confinement. "Give me water, *mizu o kudasai.* Give me water, *mizu o kudasai,*" he gasped alternately.

There! He could smell it. Yes, there was a bridge in front of him. Below a bridge a river flows. In a river there's water. The thought turned over in his mind like a spell, and pushed his legs on.

It was a strange bridge. One part stretched from his side of the river to the other. But in the middle another bridge branched off to an island forming a *T*. The island was in flames, too, and black figures seemed to be piled on the stone steps leading from the island down into the river. The water glowed a murky white, blackened in places by piles of debris. You have to get down there, he told himself. There's water there. He started onto the bridge, but something stopped him dead in his tracks. "Ghosts," he gasped.

Hundreds of figures were surging toward the bridge from the other side of the river. Yet, they were not human. Their faces were burned, covered in blood, soot, and mud. Skins peeling, their charred fragments of clothing clinging to them, he could not tell whether they were male or female, old, young, or infants, or whether they were even human at all. They all groped their way toward him.

He glanced behind and there, too, was an unbroken line of figures with burned faces and peeling skin. They were in front and behind. Suddenly he could see himself as one of them—a phantom-like figure in that line of unearthly figures fumbling forward. For the first time he felt afraid and his fright escaped in a loud moan.

Two of the figures in front of him turned around. Their faces were charred and they had lost their hair, but he could see from their height that they were children. They stopped and looked at him, and then their disfigured mouths dropped open. Shaking, they almost lost their footing. "America," the one on the right uttered. Then the one on the left opened his mouth and spoke English—not the broken English of the guard, but the English of his homeland. He remembered the little brother of the Indian maid at Susan's house back at White Sands whom he had teased about looking like a Jap. "You a Jap?" he joked, but the boy had scowled and said nothing.

This boy's painfully uttered words had the opposite meaning, though. "You American?" He had an uncanny resemblance to the Indian boy—like the Indian boy's ghost. "You American?" the Indian boy–ghost gasped again, as if it were his last breath. The line of ghosts turned. "America," they groaned from their tattered mouths. Their groans merged into one huge cry that rose into the dark sky like the raging flames, and they surged at him like a collapsing castle wall.

"Run!" a voice cried. He could not tell if it was Will's voice or a voice from heaven. "Run, son! This is your desert." For an instant he thought he saw the silver streak of a coyote leading the way across White Sands.

But it was too late. Ghosts set upon a ghost. With their last reserves of strength they flung themselves upon him. Dying piled on top of the dying. With all his remaining strength he tried to push them off and tear himself away, but they continued to pile up on him. At the bottom of the heap, there was no voice to be heard, either from Will or from heaven. Unable to breath, and in excruciating pain, he heard the sound of the crackling flames and breathed their smell. I'm going to be burned with all the bodies on top of me, he thought. Some were already dead, for the smell of death reached his nose. The coyote was gone. They were alone, figures in the pile striving with the last of their energy to gain life or deny it. The flames roared overhead. He closed his eyes.

"Why . . . ?" His consciousness was fading. "Why am I here? Why are we . . . ?" His thoughts stopped at the plural pronoun. Rain began to fall on the pile of waste. It was a black, grimy rain.

*   *   *

# III

I suppose everybody thinks I'm going to die soon. That's not surprising. I'm not sure if I want to die, but I don't think I'll last another month in this rundown ward of this rundown charity hospital, surrounded by these grumpy nurses and wheezing old fogies.

I was brought in here a month ago. They found me lying in the street. At least that's what's written on their records. I was actually sitting down in protest in front of the state governor's residence. I was sick at the time but did it anyway. I must have collapsed, because an ambulance picked me up and brought me here. I arrived in the middle of the night and the doctor on duty, Dr. Meyer (twenty-eight years old and a doctor for all of six months), took a quick look at me and decided that I must have lung cancer. "That's right, he knew as soon as he looked at you," chirped Sister Chapman, who seems to have a secret affection for him. "But you have nothing to worry about. He's working as hard as he can to cure you. Don't you forget to pray, now."

"Yes, I'll pray. I'll pray a lot," I always reply. After that, depending on her mood, she says either "You really are a good person" or "Dr. Meyer really is a good doctor." Then she smiles and, putting on an air, pushes her sliding eyeglasses back to the bridge of her nose.

Dr. Meyer, with his white skin and fair hair, is a rarity in this ancient hospital for the poor, this timeworn twelve-story legacy of the nineteenth century. The place is full of black doctors: Harlem blacks, southern blacks, Puerto Ricans, Caribbean blacks, Panamanians, Africans from Ethiopia and the Congo—lacquer-black, dark black, light black, chocolate-colored; anyway, black is black, niggers are niggers. Then there are the yellow-skins: Chinks, Japs, Flips, Vietnamese gooks, Korean gooks. . . . Whites usually have things their own way because of their color, but here it's a different world, and because he's a newcomer and probably not very good at his job, Dr. Meyer keeps a low profile. Not only are the colored doctors on top, merciful God has bestowed the gift of poverty bountifully on blacks and yellows—the bulk of the patients—so that they can have white nurses like Sister Chapman running around after them and even changing their bedpans.

The white nurses aren't here because they couldn't get a job anywhere else. Unlike the white doctors, they're at this dump as servants of God, angels come to save the souls of the pitiful colored wretches. They clean the dirty toilets and the bed pans as a testimony of their piety; but they do it all in silence with expressionless faces. Nurses like Sister Black—her face matches her name—might offer their prayers, but they aren't as pious. "How did you get so filthy?" she snaps, and slaps my behind like a bossy older sister. Unlike the doctors, the white nurses outnumber the black nurses. Maybe that's why Sister Chapman can be so smug, and why Sister Black, despite her size, keeps her head down.

When they carried me into the emergency ward on a stretcher that night, I heard Dr. Meyer ask, "I wonder what country he comes from?"

"I wonder," echoed the bespectacled Sister through her mask. I made them both jump back in surprise.

"This is my country," I informed them through my few remaining teeth. "My people were here *long* before yours." I don't know if they were shocked because a sick man on death's door had suddenly opened his mouth or because of the words themselves.

"What?" the baby-faced doctor exclaimed. (It's probably that baby face that makes him so popular with the nurses. Even Sister Black turns red like a young girl in front of him. I've never seen a blushing black face like that before.) Sister Chapman recovered first.

"He's an Indian, Doctor," she said with a smug teacher's air. "Right?" she turned to me for confirmation. I've never liked being called that name the whites have forced on us.

"No!" I shouted. I told them the name of my tribe, but the foolish woman didn't understand; she won't until the day she dies.

"He doesn't have feathers in his hair," the pea-brained doctor said diffidently, as if afraid Sister Chapman would scold him. He's obviously watched too many Westerns. He expects to see a half-naked brave with feathers in his hair and a long spear, going out on a scalping expedition. He'll never change either.

Dr. Winslow, on the other hand, as black as Sister Black and twenty years older than Dr. Meyer, isn't so stupid. When I told him the name of my tribe, he knew what I was talking about, and even the tribes we get along with and don't get along with. He was born in the Congo and went to Paris for his doctor's training. I don't know where he went off the tracks, but here he is in this hospital with fools who still think we go scalp hunting even though they live right by us.

He's a big man, arms like logs, but he doesn't use them like I did. He doesn't handle dynamite and work in thick, choking dust. He doesn't have to go into mines full of radon gas and risk getting lung cancer to bring up those lumps of uranium. He opens up the chests of the victims like me. I'm his tenth Indian lung cancer patient from the uranium mines, he says, looking down at me with sad elephant eyes that tell what happened to the other nine.

"The dust in the shafts was so thick, I could hardly open my eyes. The white bosses shouted at us from outside to get down in there. If we were too slow they pushed us down, like slaves. You work there for a while and you start to throw up. You cough up black stuff." Whenever I start complaining Dr. Winslow holds his big black hands up: "I've heard that before—from you and the nine others before you." But he still listens with his elephant ears.

"Didn't you know if you did that kind of work it wouldn't do your body any good?"

"Everybody talked about it. Anyway, I always had a headache."

"So why didn't you quit?"

"They told us it would be all right. They're good with words—they fooled us. And besides, there were no other jobs."

"Hmm." Dr. Winslow nods and walks away with his shoulders stooped forward, dragging his boots. He's the best surgeon, they say, the star of the hospital. Lung cancer, stomach cancer, esophageal cancer, cancer of the bladder—all kinds of cancer in all stages of development—he operates on them all. Black and yellow doctors, freckled white nurses, shining black nurses, poverty-stricken colored patients, even whites, and the odd scalp-hunting Indian with feathers in his hair—they all wait respectfully for the scalpel of the master from the Congo. No wonder he doesn't have much time to stop and chat with a dying man like me.

After he leaves, the stage is mine. I start talking. The other patients think I'm mad. They run to the nurses' office to ask them to shut the Indian up. If you ask me, *they're* the fools. Open your eyes, you people, and you, too, our friend from Africa, Dr. Winslow, with the sad elephant eyes and big black elephant ears. . . .

The whites lied to us from the beginning. A lot of us couldn't read. It was easy to trick us into signing their papers. Yes, and what about the "tribal government" the white masters came and got some of our fools to make? They say they represent us; they rent and sell our land to the government or mining companies. You can't sell land. You can't rent it out. That pit we were digging uranium out of, isn't that the sacred mountain where Mother Earth's heart rests? You start digging it up and you upset the balance of the world. It's like going and digging up the Christians' Mount Sinai. . . .

"So how many uranium mines are there on your tribe's land?" Dr. Winslow asked me once.

"Thirty-eight. They grind up the ore and melt it down into yellow cakes. They've got five refineries for that. Soon there'll be seventy mines and twenty-four refineries. You ever seen that yellow cake?"

"No. Have you?"

"No. All I saw was dust—and a photo of a big power station. The boss said they made power from the ore I dug out." The doctor looked as if he wanted to say something. "What about you—what have you seen?" I asked.

"Me?" he cleared his throat. "I've seen your cancer cells. I cut a small tissue sample out of your lung and examined it under the microscope, and there they were, like ants swarming around a dead insect. And . . ." He faltered again.

"And a mushroom cloud. I saw it in a photo too. Big mushroom clouds over Hiroshima and Nagasaki in Japan . . . . I suppose you've heard of the atomic bomb? The ore you dug up made those mushroom clouds. It made your cancer cells too." He paused, evidently pondering the connection between my tiny cancer cells magnified thousands of times under his microscope and the huge mushroom clouds over the Jap cities.

"How many Japs died from those atomic bombs?" I asked.

"Well, I'm not certain, but . . ." He took something that looked like a small notebook out of his pocket. I thought he was going to write some numbers down, but he started pressing buttons with his big black fingers, as if he were playing. I soon realized what the object was.

"That a calculator?"

"Yes . . . it's a Ja—" He almost said *Jap*, but corrected himself. "—Japanese calculator. It must have been about two hundred and twenty-two thousand, two hundred and twenty-two."

"That many? Poor Japs."

"It wasn't only Japanese. There were people from quite a few countries—even the United States, I heard. Prisoners of war, in other words."

"Black people like you?"

"Perhaps."

"People like me?"

"Maybe." Then he appeared lost in thought again. After a while he knitted his brows and said, "I've had strange dreams lately."

"What kind of dreams?" I didn't really need to ask. People look like that when they dream of the dead.

"Of walking ghosts," he said, his big lips moving slowly.

"Jap ghosts?" Instead of nodding, he anticipated what I would ask next.

"There are black ones too. They may be black from the smoke."

"Why do they come into your dreams?"

He looked at me for a while, his eyes becoming moist. "I know very well why they appear." Before I could ask him why, he continued, "And when the black ones come, it's as if I'm coming toward myself."

As he spoke I imagined I saw a yellow figure walking toward me. And behind it was a white one. I glanced then at my skin. It had become as white as Dr. Meyer's. I was walking toward myself. I became frightened and tried to escape. "Stop!" I cried, and started running after myself. My role had changed with that cry. "Don't chase me!" I gasped, changing back again. "Don't chase me. I'm—" Before I could say *on your side,* a blinding flash and deafening roar knocked me to the ground.

I must have slept for some time in the darkness. "Wake up!" a voice shouted. "Wake up, Dr. Meyer." When I finally regained my senses and sat up, Dr. Winslow was standing before me.

"So you've been hit, too, like me," he said, taking a look around. "The world's been blown apart. There's nobody left, only ghosts."

I realized then that I couldn't see. I had only judged it was the big black man from the voice. I frantically rubbed my eyes with my fists until finally I could make out something. It was my fists coated with blood, dark, mixed with soot and mud. I turned my gaze upward. Lifting my eyes was a great effort, not just because I was injured, but because my eyes didn't want to see what was there. He was right. The world was unquestionably destroyed and burning red. Beneath the flames were countless black piles.

"What are they?" I asked, but I knew as soon as I posed the question.

"Ghosts," he said.

"Hmm." I nodded. "Jap ghosts."

"That's right. But others too."

"What others? Like me . . . ?" I was the white Dr. Meyer.

"Yes, with black skin like you."

"But I'm white. . . ."

He motioned to my right arm with his eyes. It was not white but black with blood, soot, and mud. You're black, his eyes said. I scraped frantically at my right arm until my own skin came through. "Look," I said.

"That's right, you're yellow, Mr. Peshrakai," he said.

"No, I'm Dr. Meyer. . . ."

"Yes, you're Meyer, Mr. Meyer. And you're Mr. Peshrakai. And you're Mr. Winslow, Mr. Okhotaka. . . ."

"Mr. Winslow—that's you!"

"That's right. And I'm also Mr. Okhotaka. My name over there"—he gestured with his face far beyond the raging fires—"was Okhotaka. I took the name Winslow from a phone book. . . . So I'm Winslow and Okhotaka, Mr. Peshrakai and Mr. Meyer. Oh, yes, and Sister Black and Sister Chapman too. You, too, you're Mr. Peshrakai, Mr. Winslow, Mr. Okhotaka, Mr. Meyer, Sister Black, Sister Chapman . . ."

"What are you talking about?"

"Don't you know?" His face was drawn in sorrow. "Here there are no names, no male or female, no old, young, and even no human. . . ." He lifted his face. I lifted mine, too, to the charred, black lumps thrown to the earth beneath the flames.

"Dr. Winslow, can't you do anything?" I asked, unable to take my eyes away from the ghastly sight.

He shook his head. "All I could do was treat them for burns. And I soon ran out of medicine." What can you do with people who have become stuff? his eyes said. "There are doctors among them. I'm among them. We're all just dead waste."

I hadn't noticed until then that he was injured. His clothes had been burned or blown off, and like the crouching figures in front of us, he stood naked except for some charred shreds between his legs. If it weren't for all the gore, grit, and mud, he might have been a statue at an art museum. "I don't have much time left."

"Me neither."

As if our words were a signal, the figures started to converge on us; from left, right, front, behind—from everywhere—they crawled or staggered toward us.

"They're coming," he said calmly. There was no fear in his voice.

"But . . ." I protested. "You didn't make *it* and you didn't drop *it*."

He cocked his head as if trying to catch a sound from below, then looked up. His black figure against the flickering flames suddenly looked very old.

"You're not Winslow," I blurted out. "Not the Winslow I know. You're Okho—"

"Okhotaka's father." He stole my words. I'd heard about him from Dr. Winslow. He had worked in mines in the Congo, which enabled Winslow to attend high school and receive a scholarship to an university.

"You can make a lot of money in the mines, but"—the black man stared fixedly at me—"it doesn't do your body any good. It didn't do my father any good either." He looked just like Dr. Winslow, only older and more worn. He was breathing heavily. I stared back.

"Did you dig *it* too? Dig *it* up and get lung cancer?" I wheezed.

"Did you dig *it* too? Dig *it* up and get lung cancer?" he wheezed back.

"Got lung cancer and I'm dying."

"I'm d . . ." I didn't hear whether he said *dying* or *dead*." Figures swarmed over us from all directions. We pushed the first of them off, and I shouted, "We didn't make *it*! We didn't drop *it*!" but there were too many of them. The pile of yellow, black, white, men, women, old, young, human, or whatever it was on top of us seemed to say, "But you dug *it* out, and if you hadn't dug *it* out, they wouldn't have been able to make *it*."

"What could we do? There were no other jobs. What about our children? It was the only way we could eat . . . ." Was it me or the black man who answered, or had the black man become Dr. Winslow again? "Because of that I . . ." Did he say *could become a doctor* or *became a doctor*? Or had he now changed back into the miner again? Did he say *because of that I am dying* or *am dead*? Whatever the answers, our cries were stifled by the pile on top of us and the weight of their words: "But you dug *it* up!"

"You sure had a bad dream, didn't you?" Dr. Winslow gazed down at me. He led my eyes over to the next bed, which had been vacant. There was a boy sitting up in it. He was an Indian. By the pallor of his face I knew he had the same sickness as me. "You're both—"

I shook my head. "Our tribes don't get along. I can tell by looking at him where he's from. We like to fight but they're different. They don't take up arms—fools got themselves locked up for it during the war." I turned to the boy. "You know about that, don't you?"

He didn't reply. He looked at me for a moment—not because he understood, it seemed, but because he had heard a noise. I looked up at the doctor and his nod confirmed what I had thought: there was something wrong with the boy's head.

"His father was one of those 'fools' put in prison for refusing the draft."

"He was, was he?" I looked at the boy again. He looked more Oriental than the children from my tribe, more like a Chink or a Jap. "What does he do now?"

"He's dead. He died from drinking water."

"What?"

"Yes, he died drinking water," the doctor said, looking down with compassionate eyes that reminded me of the big Jap Buddha statue I'd seen a photo of. "He drank water from the place you were working in. There's subterranean water, from millions of years back, and they pumped it up because of the mine. It ran into a river that went through the boy's village and caused the same kind of cancer you have.

"So he died from drinking that water."

"It got into their well." He looked at the boy, who was staring vacantly into space. Again, the doctor's nod confirmed my guess: the "Jap boy" could not see. "All the livestock died one by one. Since they drank water straight from the river, the cows—" He was interrupted by a groan from the blind boy. His attempt at speech was like a child's.

"Eighteen cows, five bulls, twelve calves, seven horses, and twenty sheep." He recited the list like the lines of a prayer. "All died," he chuckled. "Mommy and Daddy too."

"The water from the well wasn't as contaminated as the river, so they didn't die as quickly as the livestock, but they got cancer. I'm sure that's what made him like this too." The big black man looked at us with his Buddha-like eyes. "Most of them born in the same maternity hospital around that time are deformed. It's because of the water from your—" He corrected himself. "—from the mine you worked in." He continued, "He's the youngest of seven children. The older six are all normal. When the third boy was born, your mine—"

"The mine I was working in," I interrupted.

"—had just started up. It must have taken until the time he was born for the contamination to build up in his parents' bodies."

"But why is he in here?" I stole a glance at the boy's face.

"He has stomach cancer. I've operated on him, but . . . like his parents and their stock, the water's going to . . ." The boy groaned, as if in reply to the black man's words.

That was the beginning of our living together in the same room. My bed was next to the window, then there was his bed, and the bed nearest the door with only white sheets on it.

"What's your name?" I asked as soon as we were alone. I wasn't sure if he understood. He held his palms above his head as if he were scrutinizing them.

"Ron," he suddenly said, as if a bucket of cold water had revived him. "And you're Chuck," he added.

"Listen, Ron. My name's Dan—Dan Peshrakai."

He nodded and said again, "Chuck, you're Chuck."

One day his sister came to visit. She had long hair, and walked with a slight limp. She looked about eighteen. I was used to being called Chuck by then. It came as a surprise, though, to find out that his name wasn't Ron.

"I wonder why he says that. His name's Ralph, not Ron." She shook her head. And she wasn't Laura, as Ron called her, but Ann.

Ralph's brothers and sisters were spread out, working here and there, so they didn't have to drink that well water. Ann worked as a maid for a white family in the state capital. Sometimes she brought flowers from their garden.

"You must have a nice boss," I commented.

"I took them," she said bluntly. She wasn't much of a talker.

"Does he say funny things like 'I've seen it'?" She asked one day. Come to think of it, he did say that sometimes. I never paid much attention, but it was odd, since he was blind.

"What does he say he saw?"

"A ball of fire, brighter than anything in the world. And men dancing like crazy after they saw it."

"But he's . . . " I glanced over to his bed. He seemed to be lost in thought. "How could he have seen those things if he was born blind? You must have told him about them."

"I did not," she retorted angrily. "I didn't tell him anything of the sort. Everyone says he must have seen them in a past world. He must have gone blind from the light of that burning ball. Isn't that right, Ron?" she said, instead of calling him Ralph.

"Mm, that's right, Laura." And then to me: "Mm, that's right, Chuck."

I glanced at Laura—or Ann—then said, "What country did you come from in the last world, Ron? Were you an Indian?"

"Mm, that's right, Chuck."

"Were you a Chink, Ron?"

"Mm, that's right, Chuck."

"Were you a Jap, Ron?"

"Mm, that's right, Chuck."

"Were you a nigger, Ron?"

"Mm, that's right, Chuck."

"Were you a white?"

"Mm, that's right, Chuck."

Ann became interested.

"Were you a man, Ron?"

"Mm, that's right, Laura."

"Were you a woman, Ron?"

"Mm, that's right, Laura."

"Were you a big man, tall enough to touch the clouds?"

"Mm, that's right, Laura."

"Were you a small kid, like a rabbit running in the mountains?"

"Mm, that's right, Laura."

Ann winked and mussed Ralph's hair, just like an older sister. "You were Dr. Winslow? And Dr. Meyer . . . ?" She began saying the names of all the people at the hospital. The answers were all "Mm, that's right, Laura." "You were Sister Chapman? And Sister Black . . . ?" and finally, "You were Ann?" "That's right, Laura." "You were Dan?" "That's right, Laura."

She might have gone on but I stopped her. "In other words, you were me, right?" I said.

"Mm, that's right. . . ." he replied childishly. To our surprise, he finished not with "Chuck" but with a well-enunciated "Dan, Dan Peshrakai."

Our lives—Ralph's, or Ron's (as I called him), and mine—went on undisturbed for a while. Ron called me Chuck. Except for the fact that we were both getting weaker, nothing out of the ordinary happened. At six-thirty every morning a white or black nurse came in, shook us awake, and stuck thermometers in our mouths. That was their greeting; they didn't even say good morning. Five minutes later they came back and took the thermometers out, Ron's first, then mine, and wrote down on a sheet of paper on their boards the temperature our cancer cells were giving off. When they had gone, still without a word, I turned and spoke to my neighbor.

"Morning, Ron. You feeling okay?"

"Mm, that's right, Chuck," he always replied. He didn't say Dan Peshrakai again.

Being together all day, we talked about many things. I told him about my mother, who was the healer of our tribe, and about the sacred spring near our house where she always prayed and did her healing. I sometimes prayed with her at the marker stone, but the spring dried up when the mining company moved in and began pumping up the underground water so that they could dig out the ore.

"Something terrible's going to happen," she would say. "They're digging around in the womb of our mother. If they hack her up and take things out, she'll feel pain. Listen, she's crying out. The white man can't hear her voice, but we can." She winced, as if she heard her own mother screaming. "You can hear her, can't you?" Sure enough, I, too, heard a rumble from the bowels of the earth, like a howl of pain. "She's going to get angry and seek revenge. When she does, it'll be the end of all of us."

I told Ron what my mother had said, and he seemed to agree with her.

"Yes, that's right, Chuck," he said distinctly. Then he strained his ears, it seemed, to catch a far-off sound, his face contorted in sorrow.

"Can you hear her crying?"

"Yes, that's right, Chuck," he replied quietly but clearly.

The longer we were together—the nearer death approached—the closer I felt to him, not like a father might feel toward a son, but as an uncle to a nephew. The feeling was mutual. There was a greater intimacy in the way I called him Ron and the way he called me Chuck.

"Ron, the flowers Laura brought are pretty." I didn't call her Ann.

"That's right, Chuck."

Then he actually started calling me Uncle Chuck. But our comfortable ambience was upset by the sudden appearance of Glen Taylor, a white through and through, thrown into the Indians' den.

"Nice weather today, Ron."

"That's right, Uncle Chuck."

"It was a shame about your father getting locked up in jail, then dying, Ron."

"That's right, Uncle Chuck."

All at once the door banged open and a newcomer was wheeled in. He had just come out of an operation and was snoring loudly. Under Sister Chapman's directions, two or three nurses laid him on the bed nearest the door, then left.

"White man!" The words came to my lips.

"That's right, Uncle Chuck."

Until the anesthetic wore off about three hours later, the white man lay there quietly. Then he began to look around curiously, although he was still groggy. Lifting his turtle-like head from between the sheets, he looked Ron and me up and down.

"Geez, this room is full of gooks. The doctor's a goddamned nigger and the patients are fuckin' gooks!" he muttered. He was about sixty years old and looked to be dying of cancer too. His voice was weak and worn, all bluff and bluster. Still, cussing is cussing, and I scowled back at the turtle head sticking out from the sheets. Ron suddenly piped up, "That's right, Uncle Chuck."

Turtle-head looked surprised and growled, "When the hell did you two come to America?"

"Who, us?" I was inured to such stupid questions by now, and kept my temper. "I'm not sure, but it must have been just a bit before your great-great-grandfathers ran away from Europe. Might have been about five thousand years before them."

"What?"

When gooks or niggers tease whites and hurt their pride, they always start raising their voices, but he had just come out of an operation. He was at death's door and sounded pathetic. He got some phlegm stuck in his throat and started spluttering. Maybe he pushed the button by his pillow, or maybe whites can communicate by telepathy; in any case, Sister Chapman suddenly appeared with an instrument, took the phlegm out of his mouth with it, and went away again in a silent pantomime.

"Knock off the jokes, or else."

"I'm not joking. We put down our roots here thousands of years before your great-great-grandfathers came. Like the coyotes. You ever seen a coyote before?" He nodded weakly. From the look on his face the pain from his wound was flaring up. I went on all the same. "I should tell you my name—it's only manners, isn't it? I'm Dan—Dan Peshrakai. And that's my nephew between your bed and mine . . . ." I couldn't help grinning. "I don't know why, but he calls me Uncle Chuck. What's *your* name?"

The best thing was to keep plying him with questions. No doubt he wanted to holler his name, but it came out like a mosquito's buzz.

"Glen. My name's Glen. Sergeant Glen Taylor. I was in the Marines." I could have figured as much. One of those nasty sergeants. Always bawling at new recruits and bullying them. Most likely he wanted to do the same to us, but unfortunately for him he couldn't move and could hardly talk. The frustration was written all over his unshaven, painstricken face. He wasn't completely beaten, though. "You Indians wouldn't know, but the Marines is not like the Army, where people get called up. We all volunteer. You know, volunteer?"

I was going to tell him that my real nephew had joined the Marines, but I changed my mind. My nephew was a fool and a sergeant too. He had gone to Vietnam and lost his left arm there. Now back at home with my tribe, he looks after his hens.

"Did you go to Vietnam?"

"Sure did." The idiot perked up. "Khe Sanh . . . you know Khe Sanh?"

"Seem to remember hearing about it. But that was a long time ago. Must have been when you were young." He didn't notice my sarcasm. He was drunk on his memories. I didn't feel like listening to his exploits at Khe Sanh and interrupted him. "Where else did you go?"

"Iwakuni." I'd never heard of the place. "It's a Jap city. Big Marine base there. I . . . " He heaved a sigh and changed the subject. ". . . I've also been to Okinawa. There's a jungle there just like 'Nam for training in. New recruits went there before they got sent to 'Nam."

My nephew still called it 'Nam too. "Your arm's probably still floating around in that 'Nam place, trying to grab a woman. No wonder you don't have much luck here," I used to tease him.

"You're real nasty, Uncle," he would growl back.

"So how many people did you kill?" I sometimes asked my nephew the same question.

"Kill?" Turtle-head seemed surprised at my question. "Kill—oh, you mean gooks. You're asking me how many gooks I killed."

"I'm asking you how many people you killed."

"How should I know? Wars aren't like they used to be. The weapons are different."

"But didn't you do a body count?" I got some phlegm stuck in my throat, but a big cough managed to get it out. "That's what they always used to call it on the news. Count the number of dead bodies."

"We're not like you chicken-liver Indians. . . ." Maybe he was beaten, or maybe he simply got some more phlegm stuck in his throat, because he began gasping and reached for the button by his pillow.

"Cough it up. That's how you get rid of it." With a simple cough he had it out, but it must have hurt his stitches, and he grimaced. "Not like you chicken-liver Indians. . . ." I mimicked. How would he continue? *We're good at killing people,* or *We don't give a damn if we kill people*? Sure enough, it put him on the spot.

"You've got something against war, don't you? You use that chicken-liver law of yours so you don't have to go and fight."

"That's right . . ." said a voice from the middle bed, then there followed a name that neither I nor turtle-head knew. " . . . Joe. That's right, Joe," Ron repeated.

The sergeant's eyes met mine briefly over Ron's bed.

"I'm not Joe, I'm Glen—Sergeant Glen Taylor." He sounded irritated.

Ron gave a slight nod as he lifted his left hand above his head and examined the palm closely. Turtle-head Glen seemed relieved.

"You got it now, Ron? I'm Glen—Sergeant Glen Taylor. I was in the Marines."

"That's right, Joe."

"Listen you Indian gook. I'm Marine Sergeant Glen Taylor."

"That's right, Joe."

I started laughing. Even though I knew it would bring up phlegm, I couldn't stop. It was as if all the cancer cells in my lungs were laughing their way up. When I managed to swallow them back down I said, "It won't help, whatever you say to him. He saw a ball of fire in the last world and it blinded him. It also did something to his head. He calls me Uncle

Chuck, and his real name is Ralph, but he always calls himself Ron, so we call him that too. I reckon he must have been called Ron in the last world, and if he had an Uncle Chuck, he must have known a Joe too." Glen looked at me as if I were also crazy. "Now, Ron, you knew a Joe in the last world, didn't you?"

"That's right, Uncle Chuck."

"And what did that white man Joe do? Did he go to Vietnam and kill people?"

"That's right, Uncle Chuck."

"And because of that he got cancer, didn't he? So now he's dying."

"That's right, Uncle Chuck."

"And when he dies, the ghosts of all the people he killed in Vietnam will come and pile themselves on top of him, won't they?" I recalled the dream I had had the other night.

"That's right, Uncle Chuck."

"Joe, why don't you say something to Ron?"

"You're just like the goddamned Vietnamese." Sadly for him, his voice didn't sound very threatening.

"That's right, Joe."

The answer was anticipated, but it still irritated him. He tried harder this time. "You're just like the goddamned Vietnamese I killed."

"That's right, Joe."

"But he looks more like a Jap or a Chink than a Vietnamese to me," I ventured.

"Japs, Chinks, Koreans—they're all the same. They're all Commie gooks. Us Marines walked all over them in the Korean War. We let the bastards have it. Before that—" He coughed. He didn't look much like the glorious Marine who walked all over them now. He spat the phlegm onto the floor, but the effort weakened him, and a trail of dribble hung from his mouth.

"Before that it was the Japs. Makin, Tarawa, Iwo Jima, Okinawa. . . . We Marines—"

"Killed thousands, eh?" I interrupted again.

"That's right, Uncle Chuck."

"Don't you understand?" he hissed. "Kill them or be killed. That's what wars are all about."

"That's right, Joe." Ron's words were enough to take the wind out of the biggest windbag. Glen suddenly became quiet.

"Kill or be killed. Both sides must be thinking that, so both are killing and being killed. The killers are killed," I mused. There was no response from the far bed.

"Huh, he's gone to sleep," I said, half to myself.

"That's right, Uncle Chuck," responded Ron.

"Probably dreaming about killing some Japs or Koreans or Vietnamese."

"That's right, Uncle Chuck."

That was how the three of us—two dying Indians and one dying white—started living together in the same room in that dingy hospital. It must have been a great blow to the pride of honorable Sergeant Glen Taylor to be put in the same room as two Indians, penniless and immobile though he was. First thing every day he would bawl, "Wake up gooks, it's morning." Ron would say his bit—"That's right, Joe"—and the day would begin. It was punctuated at times with "When I was in the Marines . . ." About the only thing he had to boast about that we didn't have—apart from his white skin and red hair—was the fact that he had been in the Marines. He bragged about how he had put the uppity young recruits in their place when he was in charge of training, the hell he used to give the draftees in Okinawa, and of course how many gooks he'd killed in Vietnam. "You don't understand. Kill or be killed—that's what war's all about."

Oh, there was one more thing he could boast about: his medal—a Purple Heart or some such thing. I finally did tell him about my idiot nephew who had lost his left arm in Vietnam. Either he didn't know there were Indians in the Marines, or he didn't want to know; in any case, he made a face as if something sour had been forced into his mouth. He spat it back out. "Listen, I wasn't a run-of-the-mill Marine. . . ." He fished around under his bed and came up with a old, dirty bag. From it he produced a tinny-looking medal. "Take a look at this. It's a Purple Heart. They only give it for very distinguished service. They don't give it to every Tom, Dick, and Harry."

"They give it to you if you kill a certain number of people, do they?" I countered.

He was either drunk on the memory of receiving his medal or else worn out from the effort of getting the bag from under his bed, because his voice sounded faint. "I didn't get this for killing a few little gooks. I got it for—" He broke off in mid-sentence and glanced fearfully at the door.

"What's the matter? Afraid someone's at the door listening to your stupid bragging? Soviet spy, eh? Or maybe the F.B.I.'s after you, afraid you're going to give away a big secret," I teased him.

I expected him to bellow back "Fuckin' gook!" but he was clearly flustered.

"What did you get it for, then?" I asked, but he deliberately changed the subject and began babbling on about Vietnamese women.

"Their skin is really something. When you hold them they snuggle up so nice," he chattered. When people start talking about the opposite sex it usually ends up meaning nothing. Maybe pimply faced kids like to listen to such talk, but I wasn't interested, especially coming from a dying, wizened old man. He went on to Jap women and Okinawan women—two completely different species, he claimed, as different as hard, moldy-bread Russian women and soft, doughnut French women. It became a lullaby, and I found myself nodding. He, too, petered out after losing his audience and began snoring faintly. The next thing I knew, Ron was by my bed, looking down at me the way the big black man did. How did he get there? He couldn't move.

"Uncle Chuck," he said, not in his normal fumbling way but with eerie clarity. "I'm going to do a play."

"A play? What kind of play?"

"A play about a ghost."

"What kind of ghost?"

"The ghost of someone he killed."

"So you're a Vietnamese gook?"

"Yes, Uncle Chuck"—he nodded—"I'm a Vietnamese ghost."

"What's your name?"

"Nakata."

"Nakata?" A long time ago I had worked in the city at a Chinese chop suey shop, washing dishes. There was someone there called Nakata. He looked like a Chink but he was a Jap—couldn't speak Japanese. "Are you really a Vietnamese ghost?"

"That's right, Uncle Chuck."

"But Nakata is a Jap."

"That's right, Uncle Chuck."

He walked toward Glen's bed, jumped nimbly onto it, and sat astride the figure wrapped in white sheets. Then he began to squeeze the figure's neck. I just watched, not because

I knew he was acting, but because I thought it wouldn't make any difference if he killed him anyway. *Those who kill will be killed*. As the thought flashed through my mind, Ron—no, Nakata—tightened his grip.

A low voice, audible from anywhere in the room, reached my ears. "Why did you kill me? What did you have against me? You killed me without even knowing my name!"

"You were the enemy," Glen gasped. "If I hadn't killed you, you'd have killed me."

"Well," thundered the voice, "you killed me, so I'll kill you. Otherwise it's not fair." The grip around Glen's neck seemed to tighten ever so slightly more.

"You're strong," I marveled, looking on as if watching a dramatic performance. How could that small, dying body find such strength? Then I saw that Ron, or maybe it was Nakata, was not the only figure astride the body in the sheets. Just like the ghosts that had piled on top of me, there were many more on the bed, all trying to strangle Glen.

"Help!" he shouted frantically, but his voice had degenerated into his mosquito buzz. No help would come. At first he cried, "Help, Sister Chapman!" Her skin was the same color as his, after all, and about as dried out. In the end he called for Dr. Winslow and even Sister Black. But his feeble cries could not penetrate the silence of the figures on top of him. They could not get past death's door, and in the corridor outside the room not a sound was to be heard.

His cries for help eventually became pleas for mercy. "Stop. Forgive me. I didn't mean to kill you. I just . . ." He was down to his last card. "I was just obeying orders. I was a soldier. Soldiers have to obey their superiors. Th-that's what soldiers have to do, Ron." He seemed to think Ron, or the pile of ghosts on top of him, would forgive him, but the figures on top merely tightened their grip. "I . . . I was just obeying orders, Ron. I can prove it. I . . ." It sounded like his last breath.

"Sergeant Taylor," the voice boomed again. "Get up. I will give you Captain Huey Thomas's orders."

"What're you talking about, Ron? Enough's enough. You can stop your play now." I was howling with laughter. But my laughter was cut short. The figure in the sheets leaped up, sending the ones on top of him flying. Not only that, Glen—Sergeant Glen Taylor was now in full combat wear.

"Yes, sir," he snapped to attention and stood waiting for orders. He glanced at me out of the corner of his eye. "You stop your play," he bellowed. "This is not your normal run-of-the-mill exercise. We're training for a special mission and you'd better snap to it." He froze again, awaiting orders from Captain Huey Thomas. I looked around, and the sight took my breath away. All the figures that had been on top of him were now lined up and, in place of the tattered garments, had on combat uniforms.

"Ten-*shun*!" a voice rang over our heads. It paused for a second and then continued.

"Sergeant Glen Taylor, take twenty-five members of the Third Division and proceed immediately to the appointed area two miles northwest of ground zero."

"Yes, sir!" he bellowed back. "On the orders of Captain Huey Thomas, I am to take twenty-five members of the Third Division and proceed immediately to the appointed area two miles northwest of ground zero!" he repeated with practiced ease. Then he turned to us. "Well, you slimy good-for-nothings, it's on. Before we start, let me warn you, you'd better keep your chattering mouths shut—you understand?—because this is a classified, top-secret operation. Everything you see and hear, you'll forget. It's all a dream, a bad dream. You got that?"

"Yes, sir!" a shrill voice piped up.

He leered at us, then glanced at his wristwatch. "Right, let's get moving. Only ten minutes to zero hour."

I glanced at my wristwatch, and in the dim light could just make out five-twenty. Zero hour must be exactly five-thirty.

"What's the matter with you slimeballs? You want to be killed with the gooks?" He pointed at me. "Get up, meathead. How long are you going to lie there? Get up now. That's an order!"

I got up, not because I was ordered to, but because some other force compelled me. I flung off my white sheets and squeezed into the line, setting off into the gloom. Most of the others were whites, but there were a few blacks and even some like me. One black recruit named Paul said that he used to work in a bar—the Golden Eagle or Golden Hawk or something. There was a Jap too. Looking closer, I saw he was Nakata. As we trudged hastily into the darkness, I asked him where in the hell he'd disappeared to from Mr. Chin's chop suey place. He looked angry and he said something about an internment camp. I asked him if it was some kind of barracks, and he got even angrier, saying that it was something like that. There was an Indian too. It turned out to be my nephew who left one arm in Vietnam. "So you've been in the Marines all this time." "That's right, Uncle Chuck, I've been here all this time. I had no choice." He had said the same thing when he joined up. He sounded angry too. I noticed he was shaking. "Are you scared? You always talk tough, but you're afraid, aren't you?" "Yes, I am, and the only reason you're not is because you don't know what's going on. We're practicing with the real thing—a bomb that'll wipe out hundreds of thousands of gooks at a time. It's already loaded on the scaffold.

One miss and that's it for us. Look, they're all shaking." He was right. White, black, and yellow—everyone was shaking. "Look at you, Uncle Chuck, you're shaking too." My nephew managed a smile.

Our pace quickened. Then everyone ran as fast as they could. "Time's up," Glen—Sergeant Glen Taylor shouted. We were in the middle of a dark, wide desert strewn with pebbles. "There's a trench. Get in there. It's going to go off." A dark line stretched along in front of us. We dove in as fast as we could and crouched low.

"Two miles northwest of ground zero!" Sergeant Glen Taylor shouted. "Shield your eyes with your hands."

The countdown began.

"Five seconds, four, three, two, one, zero . . ." The world lit up and the earth was rent. Through my closed eyes I could see the outline of the bones in my hand. Stones, pebbles, dirt—everything under the sun—came pelting down on us. This must be the end of the world, we thought. No one cried out; we were all too afraid.

"Attack!" Glen—Sergeant Glen Taylor's voice rasped. "Come on, you cowards, get out and get them. That's an order!" We leapt out of the trench into the billowing cloud of dust and sand. Ahead we could make out the tanks, trucks, and jeeps of the "gook camp." They had already been tossed about by the fireball like giant toys, but we fired on them anyway. Then another group came from the opposite direction.

"Retreat, all of you, retreat!" Glen—Sergeant Glen Taylor shouted again. "Move it or we'll all be incinerated! We're only a hundred feet from ground zero!" He dashed and we followed. From out of nowhere, we saw a truck waiting. "Get on. We've gotta get out of here."

We piled on top of each other in the back of the truck. In the next instant, a group of white-smocked doctors or technicians appeared, took the badges off our chests, and pointed an instrument at us. There was an emission of fast clicking sounds, *rat-tat-tat-tat*.

As the truck started moving, Paul or Nakata shouted, "Who's that?" We spun around to see a black figure through the swirling desert dust staggering from the gook camp toward us.

"It's a gook ghost," someone joked, but his voice carried around the truck like a shrill scream; it did look like a gook ghost killed by the fireball—no, by us—but I saw that it was Ron.

"Shoot it!" snarled Glen—Sergeant Glen Taylor, suppressing his own fear. A shot rang out almost before he could finish. The figure crumpled to the ground. Who shot him? We all turned and looked at each other.

"It was Joe," I heard someone whisper. Joe, the white soldier and ex–ranch hand, was standing with his rifle in his hands. Suddenly he started reeling, as though he were reenacting the death of the figure he had just killed. He crumpled to the hard steel deck of the truck.

"He wasn't far enough down in the trench," a familiar voice beside me said. It was Dr. Winslow. "He must have gotten a big dose of it." His big lips were trembling.

"Judging from him . . . you never know when it'll be our turn. Someday . . ."

". . . those who kill will be killed," I said, finishing the sentence fearfully.

"I feel sorry for him too," said Dr. Winslow looking over at Glen, who had just dozed off after spending the day sounding off at us. (At least that was a sign he still had some life left in him.) "You know in the desert west of here there's a big military training ground. When the Vietnam War was still on, the

Marines did some secret training there. He was in a special squad, and I think you know what got him. You've seen his medal, haven't you—his Purple Heart? He didn't get that in Vietnam. I'm certain he got it because of that training—something to keep him quiet. But it didn't, though, when he found out he was dying of cancer. . . ." He was interrupted by a loud moan. He went over, took the dying man's arm, which was now only skin and bones, and gently squeezed his hand. Glen started breathing deeply again, and the black man returned to my side.

"He started to complain, but no one would pay any attention. No one would admit that the Marines had taken part in any such exercise. He simply got sicker and sicker until he ended up here."

"Why didn't he take them to court?" I asked, though I knew the answer.

"What good would it do? You should know better. You've been wronged by your country. Besides, he didn't have any money." The same as you, his eyes said. You complained, but no one would listen. You had no money to take it to court. And you also ended up here. "I feel sorry for him too," he said again, emphasizing the *too*.

"But he killed me, Uncle Chuck." Ron caught me by surprise.

"And those who kill will be killed," I replied instinctively.

"But the killers aren't dead yet, Uncle Chuck."

"So what do you want to do?" I said, looking at the stains on the ceiling.

"Those who are killed will kill their killers, won't they, Uncle Chuck?"

"Hmm."

"That's why I'm going to kill him, Uncle Chuck." Ron

turned to look at Glen's pain-contorted face with eyes that could not see.

"Because he killed me, Uncle Chuck."

"Hmm."

"That's why I'm going to kill you, Uncle Chuck." Now he turned and looked at my contorted face, with his eyes that couldn't see. "Because you killed me, Uncle Chuck."

"I killed you?" I cried. "You're joking."

"I'm not." He shook his head, staring right into me. "If you hadn't done the digging, they couldn't have made it, Uncle Chuck. That's how you killed me. Those who are killed will kill their killers. I'm going to kill you. If I don't, it's unjust, and injustice is wrong, Uncle Chuck."

"I . . . I . . ." I stammered. "What should I do?"

"You should kill whoever killed you, Uncle Chuck."

"He . . ." My eyes naturally turned to the other bed.

"He should kill whoever killed him, Uncle Chuck."

"And . . ." I blurted out, " . . . what will happen to the world?"

"Nothing will happen, Uncle Chuck." Ron's voice seemed to come from above. "Only, the order will be changed. People above killing people below who kill people below them—that will change. Those below will kill their killers above, Uncle Chuck." The voice now seemed to come from my feet.

The big black man looked small and far away, as if through binoculars from the wrong end. He was standing at the door, looking at us with his sad elephant's expression, only more so this time. I knew what he wanted to say. This is the end.

He injected us with painkillers. The world went very hazy, and through the haze I heard Glen's hoarse voice: "Have you brought some good news?" He had taken to saying that whenever the doctor came in. He believed that before he died the President would invite him to the White House to decorate him. The bearer of the good news would be the big black man. At first, the nigger doctor (as he always called him) would receive a telephone call from the White House and come to inform him. But later on, it changed: He became a messenger from the White House. Sometimes he was a military man, sometimes a civilian. When he was a military man, Captain Huey Thomas, now a general, would also be there to pick him up. "Yes, sir!" he frothed, and moved his arm to salute his superior. When he was a civilian, he was a recently retired famous military figure serving now as special presidential aide. "The President has invited you to the White House. Please accept this honor," he mumbled deliriously.

"Since when has a special presidential aide been a nigger? Maybe when you get to meet the President, he'll turn out to be an Indian gook!" I teased him once. The big black man overheard, and he looked from my gook face to the sunken white cheeks of Glen's face and commented, "Incidentally, I hear the Japanese leader is coming to the White House to meet with the President."

After a while Sister Chapman and Sister Black became the messengers. Well, if women can become generals or cabinet ministers, why not messengers? White smocks from the White House. My mind was deteriorating, but Glen's was going faster than mine. Eventually he took to parroting, "You've brought some good news, haven't you?" over and over without stopping. His voice became louder, as if he were summoning up all his remaining strength. Sometimes he added "Yes, sir," or "The President has invited you to the White House. Please accept this honor."

"Pain in the ass, isn't he, Ron?"

"That's right, Uncle Chuck."

Our world was losing its focus. I'm not sure whether we actually spoke or not.

"He's a fool, Ron."

"That's right, Uncle Chuck. And"—he paused—"a killer."

The big black man, through reversed binoculars, came slowly toward us. "The Japanese leader has been invited to a White House luncheon with the President tomorrow," he said again, as if picking up on Glen's theme.

"What's his name—this Jap leader?"

"I can't remember." He shook his head. "The only name I know begins with an *H*—Hirohito or something. I used to hear that name a lot when I was small, back in the Congo. Like he was the Devil." He thought for a moment. "Strange, isn't it. The President here dropped bombs over there, killing God knows how many people. He must be the Devil to them. Devil invites Devil and they have lunch at the Devil's house. He should be invited instead." He motioned to Glen and sighed deeply. "He really thinks he's going to be invited. If he's not . . ." His voice trailed off and Ron spoke:

"We should go ourselves, Uncle Chuck."

The voice came up through my feet again. "And take them a present—a present for the two Devils."

At dawn, I was awakened by someone shaking me. It was Ron. I thought I was dreaming and rubbed my eyes.

"This is no dream." He grinned. "We're flying to Washington, to the White House." His voice was crisp.

"You can see!" I exclaimed. Ron looked at me, puzzled. "I'm sick; I can't move," I said, but he took me by the arms and, with amazing strength, pulled me out of bed.

"Uncle Chuck, you used to be able to run real fast." He took my hand and started running. My legs moved faster and faster, and before long I began to pull him.

"Where's Glen?" I asked as we ran.

"He's already at the helicopter. He's so happy his dream's coming true," Ron laughed. A state rescue helicopter with a red cross painted on the body was waiting on the hospital grounds.

"Hey, you Indian gooks, glad you could make it," Glen shouted when he spotted us. Without warning he gave us both a big hug. "We're off to the White House. At last I can meet the President, who gave me this." He fingered his dangling medal.

"About time too!" the big black man's voice sounded from beside us. He no longer had a sad elephant face.

"What are you so happy about?" I teased him.

"I'm happy when I see other people happy." He smiled back.

Glen piloted the helicopter. "I'm a Marine: I can do anything," he boasted. "I did the gooks over in 'Nam in a ship like this. It'll be a piece of cake. We'll land on the big green lawn in front of the White House." He moved his body, making the medal sway. The helicopter swayed with it. "Chopper's happy too."

Glen was in uniform—not combat gear but ceremonial attire. He caught me looking at it curiously. "Sergeant Glen Taylor's the name, proceeding at once to the White House by order of the Supreme Commander of the United States Forces, His Honor the President." He beamed and promptly turned the helicopter westward.

"Hey, we're going in the wrong direction."

"No we're not. We've got to pick up the present," Ron cheerily informed me. The black man also flashed a large grin.

We flew for quite a while, and needed to make a refueling stop at one point. A suspicious police officer came to ask what we were doing. Dr. Winslow produced his I.D. card and gave what must have been a reasonable explanation. We were in a state rescue helicopter with a red cross on the side, after all. "I see," the young officer said, nodding, and went away. Then we were in the air again, flying smoothly through clear morning skies.

"We're here." I must have dozed off, for I was awakened by the black man shaking me. We were hovering just above the ground. As far as the eye could see was desert. I felt I had been there before. As we got out of the helicopter a man with an Army colonel's epaulets and two or three of his subordinates came up and shook Dr. Winslow by the hand.

"I need some soil from ground zero for research I'm doing for my patients," Dr. Winslow said to them, and showed the colonel a white slip of paper.

"After you analyze it, you'll figure out how to treat them, right?" the colonel asked, inviting confirmation.

"Yes, sir!" Instead of the black man, Glen—Sergeant Glen Taylor responded with a crisp salute. The colonel returned it.

"I'm Colonel Huey Thomas of the United States Army. Who are you?"

"Sergeant Glen Taylor of the United States Marines, sir." His Purple Heart rested on his chest.

"Indian gook Chuck, Uncle Chuck," I joined in.

"I'm Ron. I'm an Indian gook too," Ron shrilled.

A jeep took us to a building with an American flag flying above it. We waited for a while in what must have been the colonel's office, then three soldiers carried in protective clothing that looked like space suits and dumped them on the floor. With the clothes on and the full-face helmets, we looked like astronauts.

"Which planet are we flying to now?" I joked.

"To the planet Earth." The big black man's face had returned to its sad elephant expression. "Ground zero is contaminated; that's why we have to wear these." Then he changed his tone and barked, "Let's move!" The lead coffin-like box in the back of the truck rattled as we sped over the desert toward ground zero. I ventured some conversation, but the black man sat like a grouchy superior and said nothing.

We came to a stop in front of a rope. Written on a sign hanging from it were the words: NO TRESPASSING: DANGER TO LIFE. We left the driver there, took the heavy box, and walked out into the stony desert in our space suits. The black man went in front, like the commanding officer, and two of us took turns carrying the lead box. We toiled with our load until the black man's space suit suddenly stopped. "This is ground zero."

The other space suits gathered round. "It's like the moon," I murmured, half to myself, but Ron overheard.

"No, it's what's left after the fireball, Uncle Chuck."

"Dig!" the black man commanded. But there was something we had to do before we started working. We—Ron and I, then the black man and Sergeant Glen Taylor—made a circle and, aiming at ground zero, proceeded to relieve ourselves. The spray rebounded off the hard earth. When we were rid of everything bottled up inside us, we let out a cheer and burst out laughing. The ground had become softer.

"Dig, dig, let's dig it up," I shouted, "piss and all!" We set to work piling the earth into the lead coffin.

"That's it, let's go!" The black man gave the order and we took turns once more carrying the box, stumbling over the desert stones back to the truck.

Twenty minutes later we had the box in the helicopter and were airborne again. We were exhausted and said nothing for a while, but as the fatigue wore off, Glen—Sergeant Glen Taylor glanced over his shoulder at the lead coffin in the back and bawled, "We've got a damned good present for the President. We must look like Santa Claus." (Dr. Winslow had ordered us to keep our space suits on.) He seemed about to cry—maybe for joy. Tears began rolling down his hollow cheeks into the sparse stubble on his chin. His face twitched and finally took the shape of a laugh. Ron gestured that he was crazy.

After one more refueling stop, we finally approached Washington, D.C. The white highway cut a distinct line through the green trees, and the cars on it seemed to be moving at about the same speed as our helicopter.

"That's the C.I.A.," Ron called out. He pointed to a big grey building. "And there's the Pentagon." In the trees was a beige five-sided structure.

"And there's the Potomac River!" Glen—Sergeant Glen Taylor shouted, space-suited arm stretching toward the big river below and all the yachts with white sails. "Isn't it beautiful? It could only be the capital of the United States." He was beaming, all vestiges of sickness gone.

This time it was my turn. "There it is!" I recognized the white, sugar-candy building from photographs I'd seen.

"We're here, we're here," Glen—Sergeant Glen Taylor blubbered. "Steady," Ron cautioned, but he carried on, almost delirious. "We've come to meet the President. We've brought him a present!" The fresh emerald-green lawn rolled out in front of the picture-perfect white building. There were two flag poles, one carrying the Stars and Stripes, the other white with a red circle. "Mr. President, Supreme Commander of the United States Forces. I, Sergeant Glen Taylor, have duly arrived this day in compliance with your orders. . . ." He began to remove his space suit. The black man, who had been quiet until then, reached out and stopped him.

"Wait, we're going to meet the President and his guest in this. We've got to be dressed properly for the occasion. It's etiquette." Two men were walking slowly from the White House toward a rostrum in the middle of the green lawn. Both were wearing black tuxedos. "They should be wearing ceremonial dress like us. It would be more appropriate," he said under his breath, and beat the breast of his space suit like a mad gorilla. "We have a suitable present for the occasion. . . ." He glanced back at the lead coffin. "We'll tip that box of dirt on the lawn down there. It'll get a lethal dose in an instant."

"And then?" I asked.

"The killers will be killed," Ron said for him.

"The killers will be—"

"That's right, Uncle Chuck," Ron said in his hospital bed voice. "The order of the world will change from the bottom."

People on the lawn had noticed the helicopter and were looking up.

"There's the President. Mr. President, Supreme Commander of the United States Forces," Glen—Sergeant Glen Taylor bawled hysterically. "The Jap boss is there too." The two men seemed to be helping each other onto the rostrum. "What's his name?"

The black man had said before that it began with an *H*. I tried to say it, but it came out as *Hiroshima*.

"Quiet. Land over there!" the black man hissed.

"Yes, sir!" Glen—Sergeant Glen Taylor moved the stick adroitly. The machine descended. The figures on the rostrum became bigger and bigger. Music reached our ears. Suddenly the helicopter jolted and plunged us and the lead coffin toward the rostrum. The band was playing the national anthem. Glen—Sergeant Glen Taylor of the United States Marines had unwittingly taken his hand off the stick and tried to stand.

"We're going to hit them. We're going to kill them!" I cried.

"That's right, Uncle Chuck, the order of the world will change from the bottom."

Dr. Winslow slowly lifted his sad elephant face from the beds. "They're dead," he sighed. "All of them, dead."

It is only materialistic people who seek to make shelters. Those who are at peace in their hearts already are in the great shelter of life. There is no shelter for evil. Those who take no part in the making of world division by ideology are ready to resume life in another world, be they of the Black, White, Red or Yellow race. They are all one, brothers.

—A Hopi prophecy,
from *The Book of the Hopi*
by Frank Waters